桑德拉·希斯内罗丝
Sandra Cisneros

芒果街上的小屋
The House on Mango Street

译林出版社

突然间黄昏变得明亮，
因为此刻正有细雨在落下，
或曾经落下。下雨
无疑是发生在过去的一件事。

谁听见雨落下，谁就回想起
那个时候，幸福的命运向他呈现了
一朵叫做玫瑰的花
和它奇妙的、鲜红的色彩。

这蒙住了窗玻璃的细雨
必将在被遗弃的郊外
在某个不复存在的庭园里洗亮
架上的黑葡萄
　　……

——博尔赫斯《雨》

目录
CONTENTS

序:回忆是实体的更高形式	1
芒果街上的小屋	3
头发	6
男孩和女孩	8
我的名字	10
猫皇后凯茜	15
我们的好日子	17
笑声	21
吉尔的旧家具买卖	23
么么·奥提兹	27
路易、他的表姐和表兄	29
玛琳	32
那些人不明白	34
有一个老女人她有很多孩子不知道怎么办	35

37	瞧见老鼠的阿莉西娅
41	大流士和云
43	还有……
51	小脚之家
56	米饭三明治
60	塌跟的旧鞋
63	髋骨
70	第一份工
75	黑暗里醒来的疲惫的爸爸
77	生辰不吉
83	伊伦妮塔、牌、手掌和水
88	没有姓的杰拉尔多
93	埃德娜的鹭鸶儿
97	田纳西的埃尔
99	塞尔
105	四棵细瘦的树
107	别说英语
110	在星期二喝可可和木瓜汁的拉菲娜
112	萨莉
115	密涅瓦写诗
117	阁楼上的流浪者
119	美丽的和残酷的
123	一个聪明人
125	萨莉说的

猴子花园	129
红色小丑	135
亚麻地毡上的玫瑰	137
三姐妹	139
阿莉西娅和我在埃德娜的台阶上交谈	143
一所我自己的房子	145
芒果有时说再见	149

The House on Mango Street	151
Hairs	155
Boys & Girls	157
My Name	159
Cathy Queen of Cats	161
Our Good Day	163
Laughter	167
Gil's Furniture Bought & Sold	169
Meme Ortiz	172
Louie, His Cousin & His Other Cousin	174
Marin	177
Those Who Don't	180
There Was an Old Woman She Had So Many	

182	Children She Didn't Know What to Do
184	Alicia Who Sees Mice
186	Darius & the Clouds
188	And Some More
193	The Family of Little Feet
198	A Rice Sandwich
202	Chanclas
205	Hips
211	The First Job
215	Papa Who Wakes Up Tired in the Dark
217	Born Bad
223	Elenita, Cards, Palm, Water
227	Geraldo No Last Name
230	Edna's Ruthie
234	The Earl of Tennessee
237	Sire
240	Four Skinny Trees
242	No Speak English
246	Rafaela Who Drinks Coconut & Papaya Juice on Tuesdays
248	Sally
252	Minerva Writes Poems
254	Bums in the Attic
256	Beautiful & Cruel

A Smart Cookie	258
What Sally Said	260
The Monkey Garden	262
Red Clowns	269
Linoleum Roses	271
The Three Sisters	273
Alicia & I Talking on Edna's Steps	277
A House of My Own	279
Mango Says Goodbye Sometimes	280

漫步芒果街	283
青芒果之味	295
那些幸福的小雨点	299
感谢	302

回忆是实体的更高形式
代译序

陆谷孙

首次看到译文,据说出自某位"海归"之笔,果然文字清通,读来亲切,兼有详尽注解助读。此书编辑知我喜读,一阵穷追猛打,邀我作序,只好请她把原文寄来。越一日,果有快递上门,把希斯内罗丝的 *The House on Mango Street* 寄达,薄薄的40页文字,附前后两幅插图,第一幅以黑白色调为主,上有尖顶旧屋,有东倒西歪的庭院护栅,有矮树,有月亮,有黑猫,有奔逃中回头的女孩,清澈的大眼睛,表情羞涩中略带惶惑;后一幅跃出大片亮黄,俯角下的女孩身影不成比例地拖长到画面之外,画的底部是小朵孤芳,一样拖着阴影。被插图所吸引,我开卷读文字,那原是个"愁多知夜长"的日子,本不想读书写字,可一口气读完这位美国墨裔女作家的中篇,如一川烟草激起满城风絮,竟不由自主地跳出肉身的自我,任由元神跃到半空中去俯察生活·童年、老屋、玩伴、亲人、"成长的烦恼"、浮云、瘦树、弃猫、神话……

2

我喜欢这部作品,首先是因为希斯内罗丝女士以日记式的断想,形诸真实的稚嫩少女文字,诗化了回忆。就像黑格尔所言,回忆能保存经验,回忆是内在本质,回忆是实体的更高形式。当我读着作品,感到元神跃出肉身时,应验的正是黑格尔的这些话。近年来,随着反对欧洲中心主义思潮的蔓延,美国文坛另类少数族裔作家(尤其是女作家)的话语空间已远非昔日可比,重要性日渐凸现。开始时,他或她们的回忆或多或少无不带有一种蓄积已久的愤懑;渐渐地,正如米兰·昆德拉所言,"在夕阳的余晖下,所有的一切,包括绞刑架,都被怀旧的淡香所照亮",多元文化业已是一个文化既成事实,少数族裔作家的作品里也便开始渗入丝丝的温馨暖意,可以说是以一种 mellowness 在化解最初的 bitterness。我读过也教过美籍华裔作家的《女武士》、《唐人》、《喜福会》等作品,拿这些作品与希斯内罗丝的《芒果街上的小屋》作一个比较,上述趋势可以看得比较明白——当然在美华人与墨人的移入方式、人数、作为、地位、对母国文化的认同感等等不尽相同。但回忆成为悲怆中掺加了醇美,从审美的角度看,似更接近"实体的更高形式",而把场景从麻将桌移到户外,视界也扩展了。

我喜欢这部作品的另一个原因是,正像插图中女孩的眼神,始而回眸，最后怯生生地仰望，作品糅合了回忆和等待。美墨聚居区的少女带上她的书远行了，据她说"我离开是为了回来。为了那些我留在身后的人。为了那些无法出去的人"。（见小说最后三短句）我说"等待"，不说"展望"，是因为像《等待戈多》一样，前一用词拓启了一个开放性的不定阈：忧乐未知，陌阡不识，死生无常，人生如寄；不像"展望"那样给人留下一条光明的尾巴。非此，经验性的回忆无由升华到形而上的哲理高度。笔者渐入老境，虽说一生平淡，也渐悟出"我忆，故我在"和"我等，故我在"的道理。当然，等待什么，那是不可知的。

作品中少数族裔青少年的英语让人耳目一新，本身就是对主流话语的一种反叛。"超短式"的句法（如以"Me"代"As for me"）、不合文法的用语、屡屡插入的西班牙语专名和语词，可以说是族裔的专用符号。除此之外，书中英文由抑扬格的音部和兴之所至的散韵造成的韵律之美，尤为别致，有些段落晓畅可诵。无怪乎，虽有争议，作品会被选作教材，而且受到某些传统主义文评家的褒评。

芒果街上的小屋

芒果街上的小屋

我们先前不住芒果街。先前我们住鲁米斯的三楼。再先前我们住吉勒。吉勒往前是波琳娜,再前面,我就不记得了。我记得最清楚的是,搬了好多次家。似乎每搬一次,我们就多出一个人。搬到芒果街时,我们有了六个——妈妈、爸爸、卡洛斯、奇奇、妹妹蕾妮和我。

芒果街上的小屋是我们的,我们不用交房租给任何人,或者和楼下的人合用一个院子,或者小心翼翼别弄出太多的声响,这里也没有拿扫帚猛敲天花板的房东。可就算这样,它也不是我们原来以为自己可以得到的那样的房子。

4

　　我们得赶紧搬出鲁米斯的公寓。水管破了,房东不愿来修理,因为房子太老。我们得快快离开。我们借用着邻居的卫生间,用空的牛奶壶把水装过来。这就是为什么爸妈要找房子,这就是为什么我们搬进了芒果街上的小屋,远远地,从城市的那一边。

　　他们一直对我们说,有一天,我们会搬进一所房子,一所真正的大屋,永远属于我们,那样我们就不用每年搬家了。我们的房子会有自来水和好用的水管。里面还有真正的楼梯,不是门厅台阶,而是像电视上的房子里那样的楼梯。我们会有一个地下室和至少三个卫生间,那样洗澡的时候就不用告诉每个人。我们的房子会是白色的,四周有树木,还有一个很大的院子,草儿生长着,没有篱笆把它们圈起来。这是爸爸手握彩票时提到的房子,这是妈妈在给我们讲的睡前故事里幻想着的房子。

　　可是芒果街上的小屋全然不是他们讲的那样。它很小,是红色的,门前一方窄台阶,窗户小得让你觉得它们像是在屏着呼吸。几处墙砖蚀成了粉。前门那么鼓,你要用力推才进得来。这里没有前院,只有四棵市政栽在路边的小榆树。屋后有个小车库,是用来装我们还没买的小汽车的,还有个小院子，夹在两边的楼中间，越发显得小了。我们的房子里有楼梯，可那只是普通的门厅台阶，而且房子里只有一个卫生间。每个人都要和别人合用一间卧房——妈妈和爸爸、卡洛斯和奇奇、我和蕾妮。

我们住在鲁米斯时，有一回学校的嬷嬷经过那里，看到我在房前玩。楼下的自助洗衣店被用木板封了起来，因为两天前刚被洗劫过。为了不走掉生意，主人在木头上涂抹了几个字："是的，我们在营业"。

"你住在哪里呀？"她问。

那里。我说，指了指三楼。

你住在那里？

那里。我不得不朝她指的地方看去——三层楼上，那里墙皮斑驳，窗上横着几根木条，是爸爸钉上去的，那样我们就不会掉出来。你住在那里？她说话的样子让我觉得自己什么都不是。那里。我住在那里。我点头。

于是我明白，我得有一所房子。一所真正的大屋。一所可以指给别人看的房子。可这里不是。芒果街上的小屋不是。目前就这样，妈妈说。这是暂时的，爸爸说。可我知道事情是怎样的。

头发

我们家里每个人的头发都不一样。爸爸的头发像扫把,根根直立往上插。而我,我的头发挺懒惰。它从来不听发夹和发带的话。卡洛斯的头发又直又厚。他不用梳头。蕾妮的头发滑滑的——会从你手里溜走。还有奇奇,他最小,茸茸的头发像毛皮。

只有妈妈的头发,妈妈的头发,好像一朵朵小小的玫瑰花结[1],一枚枚小小的糖果圈儿,全都那么拳曲,那么漂亮,因为她成天给它们上发卷。把鼻子伸进去闻一闻吧,当她搂着你时。当她搂着你时,你觉得那么安全,闻到的气味又那么香甜。是那种待烤的面包暖暖的香味,是那种她给你让出一角被窝时,和着体温散发的芬芳。你睡在她身旁,外面下着雨,爸爸打着鼾。哦,鼾声、雨声,还有妈妈那闻起来像面包的头发。

1 玫瑰花结是指玫瑰花状的圆形花饰。

男孩和女孩

男孩和女孩生活在不同的世界。男孩在他们的天地里,我们在我们的天地里。比如我的弟弟们。在家里,他们有很多话跟我和蕾妮说。可是到了外面,他们就不能被人家看见和女孩说话。卡洛斯和奇奇是彼此最要好的朋友……不是我们的。

蕾妮还很小,做不了我的朋友。她只是我的妹妹,这不是我的错。你不能挑选妹妹,你只是就那么得到了她们,某些时候她们就像蕾妮一样到来。

她不能去和法加斯家的孩子们玩,要不然,她会变得和他们一样。既然她跟在我后面来了,她就是我的责任。

有一天,我会有一个我自己的、最要好的朋友。一个我可以向她吐露秘密的朋友。一个不用我解释就能听懂我的笑话的朋友。在那之前,我将一直是一个红色气球,一个被泊住的气球[2]。

---

[2] 在这个故事里,气球是向外逃逸的象征,而"被泊住"的状态暗示了某种束缚,比如她与蕾妮的关系意味着的家庭责任。

我的名字

在英语里,我名字的意思是希望。在西班牙语里,它意味着太多的字母[3]。它意味着哀伤,意味着等待。它就像数字九[4]。一种泥泞的色彩。它是每到星期天早晨,爸爸刮胡子时播放的墨西哥唱片,呜咽似的歌。

它过去是我曾祖母的名字,现在是我的。她也是一个属马的女人,和我一样,生在中国的马年——如果你生为女人,这会被认为是霉运——可是我想,这是个中国谎,因为,中国人和墨西哥人一样,不喜欢他们的女人强大。

我的曾祖母。要是我见过她多好,女人中的野马,野得不想嫁人。直到我的曾祖父用麻袋套住她的头把她扛走。就那样扛着,好像她是一盏华贵的枝形吊灯。那就是他的办法。

后来,她永远没有原谅他。她用一生向窗外凝望,像许多女人那样凝望,胳膊肘支起忧伤。我想知道她是否随遇而安;是否会为做不成她想做的人而伤怀。埃斯佩朗莎。我继承了她的名字,可我不想继承她在窗边的位置。

在学校里,他们说我的名字很滑稽,音节好像是铁皮做的,会碰痛嘴巴里的上颚。可是在西班牙语里,我的名字是更柔和的东西做的,像银子,没有妹妹的名字那么浑厚。她叫玛格达蕾娜,这名字没我的美。玛格达蕾娜回到家里可以叫成蕾妮。可我总是埃斯佩朗莎。

我想要取一个新的名字,它更像真正的我,那个没人看到过的我。埃斯佩朗莎换成黎桑德拉或者玛芮查或者泽泽 X。一个像泽泽 X 的名字就可以了。

---

3 英文单词"letter"既可以作"字母"解,也可以作"信"解。太多的信,意味着等待。通过这层隐义,句子前后意义得以贯通。
4 作者说,9 是 10 之前的那个数字,是变化之前的数字。她选用这个数字来传达一种等待的意味,因为"我",是一个即将成年的孩子,在等待改变,等待成熟和绽放。

15

猫皇后凯茜 [5]

她说,我是法兰西皇后的远远远房表亲。她住在楼上,那边,那个"捉小孩的人"乔的隔壁。离他远点,她告诉我说,他很危险。街角那家小店是宾尼和布兰卡的。他们还蛮好,可只是靠在糖果柜台上时才对你好。两个像老鼠一样邋遢的女孩住在街对面。你不会想去认识她们的。埃德娜是你家隔壁房子的主人。她过去有幢大得像鲸鱼的房子,可她弟弟把它卖了。他们的妈妈说,别,别呀,千万别卖。我不会的。可后来她一闭眼,他就卖了它。阿莉西娅自从上了大学就傲气起来了。她过去挺喜欢我,可现在不了。

16

猫皇后凯茜养了好多好多好多好多猫。猫宝宝、大个猫、瘦猫、病猫。睡姿像个面包圈的猫。爬到冰箱顶上的猫。在餐桌上散步的猫。她的房子就像个猫天堂。

你想要个朋友。她说,好的,我会做你的朋友,可只能做到下星期二,那时我们就得搬走了,不得不搬了。然后,她似乎忘了我才搬进来,说,这个社区的人越来越杂了。

凯茜的父亲有一天会要飞到法国去,找到远方的、她父亲那边的远远远房表亲,去继承家宅。我是怎么知道这些的呢?是她告诉我的。同时,他们要从芒果街向北搬迁,离开这里一点路,在每次像我们这样的人家不断搬进来的时候。[6]

---

5 在刘易斯·卡洛尔的《爱丽丝镜中奇遇记》中,有这样一节:爱丽丝一梦醒来,发现纸牌皇后变成了她的小猫。卡洛尔是对作者影响颇深的作家。此篇或许是个例证。在这里,小姑娘凯茜的绰号,以及她自称和法兰西皇后的亲缘,都暗合了卡洛尔童话中的情节。因此,凯茜、猫和皇后的关联指向一个暗嵌的典故。这既是对自己喜爱的大师的致礼,也延伸了作品的内涵。

6 要明白这段话,需了解上世纪六十年代的社会背景:在芝加哥,因为文化、经济和种族等方面的差异,相对贫困的拉美裔移民大量拥入某个社区,原来居住在这里的白人就会选择搬迁,到以白人为主的社区里去。

我们的好日子

如果你给我五块钱,我会永远做你的朋友。那个小的这么对我说。

五块钱很便宜,因为我没有任何朋友,除了凯茜,她是我星期二之前的朋友。

五块钱,五块钱。

她想找人凑钱,那样,她们可以从那个叫提陀的小孩那里买一辆自行车。她们已经有十块了,她们再添五块钱就够了。

只要五块。她说。

别和他们说话。凯茜说,你难道看不出来他们闻起来像扫把?

可是我喜欢她们。她们的衣服又皱又旧。她们穿着锃亮的礼拜天的鞋子,却没穿短袜。鞋子把她们的光脚踝擦得红红的。我喜欢她们。尤其是那个大的,笑的时候露出一口牙齿。我喜欢她,尽管她让小的出来说话。

五块,小的说,只要五块。

凯茜在拽我的胳膊,我知道,接下来我不管做什么,都会让她永远生我气的。

等等。我说着跑到屋里拿了五块钱。我自己存有三块,又拿了蕾妮两块。她不在家,可我肯定,她发现我们有辆自行车会很高兴的。我回来的时候,凯茜走了,我知道她会这么做,可我不在乎。我有了两个新朋友和一辆自行车。

我叫露西。大的说。这是我妹妹拉切尔。

我是她妹妹。拉切尔说。你是谁?

我希望我的名字是卡桑德拉,或者阿乐克西丝,或者玛芮查——只要不是埃斯佩朗莎,什么名字都可以。可我告诉她们我的名字的时候,她们没有笑。

我从得克萨斯来,露西说着咧嘴一笑。塔是在这里出生的,而我在得克萨斯。

你是说她吧。我说。[7]

不,我是从得克萨斯来。她没听明白我的意思。

这辆车我们三个这么分配吧,拉切尔已经想在前面了。今天是我的,明天是露西的,后天是你的。

可每个人都想今天骑,因为车是新的。于是我们决定从明天开始轮流。今天它属于我们大家。

我还没有告诉她们蕾妮的事。事情太复杂了。尤其是,为了谁第一个骑的问题,拉切尔差点把露西的眼睛挖出来。最后我们同意一块骑,为什么不呢?

露西腿长,她来踩踏板。我坐在后座上,拉切尔足够苗条,她坐到了前杠上,弄得车子一个劲摇晃,好像轮子是实心意粉做的。不过一会儿我们就习惯了。

我们越骑越快,骑过了我的家,那破落又悲哀、墙砖碎裂的红色小屋,骑过了街角宾尼先生的小卖铺,骑在了危险的大道上。自助洗衣店、旧货店、药店、一个个窗子、一辆辆汽车,越来越多的汽车,都经过了。我们围着街区绕了一圈,骑回芒果街。

巴士上的人向我们挥手。一个很胖很胖的女人边过街边说,你们的装载量很大呀。

拉切尔喊道,你的装载量也很大呀。她说话好冒失。

我们沿着芒果街前行。拉切尔、露西、我,还有我们的新自行车。歪歪扭扭的回程上,我们一直笑呀笑。

7　露西话里的"塔"的原文是宾格代词"her",按正确的用法,应该用主格。所以埃斯佩朗莎纠正她,应该用主格"she",也就是"她"。

笑声

蕾妮和我看起来不像姐妹……不是一眼就能看出来的那种。人们可以看出拉切尔和露西是,因为她们有一模一样的雪糕似的厚嘴唇,她们家所有人的嘴唇都是那样的。可我们不是那种像法。我和蕾妮,我们相像的地方比你能看到的多。比如我们的笑声。不是拉切尔和露西一家人那样羞涩的傻笑,像冰淇淋铃声[8]一样,而是突然的、吃惊的笑,像一叠盘子打碎了的感觉。还有其他一些我没法说清楚的地方。

一天我们经过一座房子,我心想,它看起来像我过去在墨西哥见过的房子。我不知道为什么。这房子和我记忆中的房子没有什么地方是一模一样的。我甚至不知道为什么我这么想。可它就是给我那种感觉。

看那房子,我说,它看着像是墨西哥的。

拉切尔和露西看着我,好像我在发傻一样。可还没等她们笑出来,蕾妮就说:没错,那就是墨西哥式的。而那恰恰是我当时的想法。

8　在美国,冰淇淋车几乎已经成为一种文化象征。销售员们会摇响铃铛在大街小巷招徕生意。

吉尔的旧家具买卖

那里有家旧货店。一个老人开的。我们有次从他那里买过一台旧冰箱。卡洛斯的一箱子杂志卖了一块钱。那铺面很小,只有一格脏兮兮的窗户透光。他从来不开灯,除非你带了买东西的钱。于是我们,我和蕾妮,在昏暗中张望,看见各种各样的物什。几张脚朝天的桌子、一排排的圆角冰箱、你一捶它就会向空中喷吐灰尘的沙发和一百台看不大起来的电视。一样东西摞在另一样上面,形成了店里一条条细长的甬道。你很容易就迷失了方向。

店主是个黑人,他不太说话。如果你不太熟悉的话,可能在里面过好长时间,才会注意到有一副金色眼镜在黑暗中游动。自以为聪明的蕾妮会和所有的老人交谈,她问他许多问题。我呢,从来没和他说过什么,除去那次花一角钱买了一个自由女神像。

可是蕾妮,我有次听到她问,这里这个是什么,老人说,这个,是音乐盒。我飞快地转身,以为他在说一个漂亮的盒子,上面印着花朵,里面有个芭蕾舞小人的那种。但老人指的地方没有那样的东西。那只是一个旧木盒,里面有一张大的黄铜录音片,上面有些小洞洞[9]。接着他启动了它,忽然间响起来千百样的声音。好像被他这一弄,有一百万只飞蛾从蒙灰的家具上,从天鹅颈状的阴影中,从我们的骨头里翻飞出来。又好像是一骨碌儿水滴。或是木琴,轻轻地一拨弦,发出如同手指滑过金属梳齿的声音。

然后我不知道为什么,不得不背过身去,装做我不是那么在意那个盒子,免得蕾妮看到我有多傻。可是蕾妮更傻,已经在问价钱,我看到她的手指伸到裤袋里摸钱去了。

这个,老人说着合上盖子,这个不卖。

---

9 音乐盒里的金属录音片,上面有洞,这些洞控制音阶,从而发出预先设置的旋律。

么么·奥提兹

凯茜一家搬走后,么么·奥提兹搬进了她的家。他其实不叫么么。他叫胡安。可我们问他叫什么名字时,他说叫么么。除他妈妈外,所有人都这么叫他。

么么有条灰眼睛的狗,一条有两个名字的牧羊犬,一个英文名一个西班牙名。那条狗很大,像一个披着狗皮的人,跑起来和主人一样,又笨又癫,脚爪踢里踏拉,一路拍打过去,像没系带的鞋。

凯茜的爸爸盖了么么搬进去住的屋子。是木头的。屋里的地面有坡度。有的房间在坡上,有的在坡下。没有小间。房子前面有21级台阶,全都向一边倾斜,盘踞在那里像一嘴歪牙(凯茜说,是故意做成这样的,方便雨水流出去)。么么的妈妈从门道里一喊,么么就手忙脚乱地爬上这21级木台阶,后面跟着爬的是那条有两个名字的狗。

屋后面是个院子,大部分地方是泥土地面,还有一扎油腻腻的木板,是过去的车库。不过,你记得最清的应该是那棵树,巨大,枝干肥硕,高高的枝丫上栖息着繁盛的松鼠家族。从上面张望,周围都是邻里的屋顶,A字形,浇了黑色的沥青。上面的天沟里,躺着一些永远不再着地的皮球。树底下,那条有两个名字的狗在冲着空气狂吠。街区的尽头是我的家,看上去更小了,像只猫儿缩起脚爪窝在那里。

这棵树被我们挑来举行第一届年度人猿泰山跳跃比赛。么么赢了。可两条胳膊都摔破了。

路易、他的表姐和表兄

么么家的楼下是一个地下室,么么的妈妈把它收拾了一下,租给了一家波多黎各人,路易一家人。路易是老大,下面全是小妹妹。他其实是我弟弟的朋友,可我知道他有两个表亲,他的T恤从不掖进裤子里。

路易家的小表姐比我们大。她住在路易家里,因为她自己的家在波多黎各。她好像是叫玛琳或玛芮斯,或者跟这差不多的名字。她总是穿暗色的尼龙丝袜,化很多妆,那是她推销雅芳的时候不花钱得来的。她没法出门——得照看路易的小妹妹们,可她常常站在门道里,一直唱着歌,打着响指。她只唱一首歌：

苹果桃儿南瓜派哟，
你在恋爱我也在哟。

路易还有一个表兄。我们只见过他一次，可那次很轰动。我们在巷子里玩排球，他开着一辆又大又气派的黄色凯迪拉克过来了，白壁轮胎，镜子上系着一条黄绶带。路易的表兄把胳膊伸在车窗外面。他摁了几下喇叭，许多张脸从路易家的后窗露出来，接着，出来很多人——路易、玛琳和所有的小妹妹们。

每个人都朝车里看，问他怎么弄来的。车里有白色地毯和白色皮座。我们都求他带我们兜兜风，并问他是从哪里弄来的。路易的表兄说上车吧。

我们每个人都得抱个路易的小妹妹在膝盖上才挤得下，可这没事儿。座位又大又软像沙发一样，汽车的后窗上有只小白猫，汽车停下或转弯的时候，它的眼睛就会变亮。车窗不像普通的车窗那样要摇上去，而是有一个按钮会自动地代你开关。我们沿着巷子兜了街区六遍。路易的表兄说,如果我们不停止玩车窗和拨弄调频收音机的话,他就要让我们走着回去。

我们第七次开进巷子的时候听到了警笛声……开始很轻,后来就很响了。路易的表兄马上就地停车,对我们说,统统下去。接着他猛踩油门,汽车飞出去变成一团黄色。我们还没反应过来,停在巷子里的警车同样飞快地追了上去。我们看到街区那头的黄色凯迪拉克想要左转弯,可我们的巷子太细了,汽车撞在了一根灯柱上。

玛琳尖叫起来,我们朝街那头跑过去,警车的警报器在那里闪着炫目的蓝光。那辆黄色凯迪拉克的鼻子皱得像美洲鳄的一样。除了流血的嘴唇和淤青的额头外,路易的表兄没什么大碍。他们给他戴上手铐,推进警车的后座。他们开走的时候我们都挥手送别。

玛琳

玛琳的男朋友在波多黎各。她给我们看他的信,并让我们答应,别告诉任何人她回波多黎各后他们就要结婚。她说他还没有找到工作,可她在靠卖雅芳和照看表妹们攒钱。

玛琳说她如果明年还留在这里的话,她要去市中心找一份真正的工作,因为最好的工作都在那里。因为你总得打扮漂亮点,穿上好衣服,才能在地铁里遇到一个会和你结婚,带你住到远方大屋里的人。

可是第二年路易的父母打算把她送回她妈妈那里,并写上一封信说她太麻烦了。这太糟糕了,因为我好喜欢玛琳。她比我大,懂得许多事情。是她告诉我们戴夫小宝的妹妹是怎么怀孕的;去掉唇髭用什么霜最好;数数你手上的小白点就能知道有多少男孩在想你;还有好多别的我现在记不起来的事情。

在玛琳的婶婶下班回家前,我们从来都看不到玛琳。在那以后,她也只能出到房子前面。她每晚都拿着个收音机在那里。等她婶婶房间里的灯熄灭后,玛琳就会点一支烟,如果那会儿外面冷,或者收音机不响,或者我们相互没话说,这些都不要紧;要紧的是,玛琳说,要让男孩子看到我们,我们看到男孩子。因为玛琳的裙子更短,因为她的眼睛很漂亮,因为她在很多方面已经比我们成熟,男孩子跑过来说一些蠢话,比如我爱上了你说是眼睛的那两个青苹果,把它们给我吧为什么不?玛琳只是看着他们,眼睛都不眨一下,也不害怕。

玛琳,街灯下独自起舞的人,在某个地方唱着同一首歌,我知道。她在等一辆小汽车停下来,等着一颗星星坠落,等一个人改变她的生活。

那些人不明白

那些不明白我们的人进到我们的社区会害怕。他们以为我们很危险。他们以为我们会用亮闪闪的刀子袭击他们。他们是些笨人,不小心迷了路走到了这里。

可我们不害怕。我们知道那个斜眼的是戴夫小宝的弟弟,站在他旁边戴着草帽的高个儿是罗莎家的埃迪·V.,而那个大个,看上去像个沉默的大人的,他是胖孩,虽然他不再胖了也不再是小孩。

到处都是棕色的人,我们是安全的。可是看看我们开进另一个肤色的街区时,我们的膝盖就抖呀抖,我们紧紧地摇上车窗,眼睛直直地看着前面。是的,情形一直一直是这样。

有一个老女人她有很多孩子不知道怎么办

罗莎·法加斯的孩子太多太过分了。那不是她的错你知道,只因为她是他们的妈妈,一个要应付这么多个。

法加斯的孩子不乖,可是只有一个妈妈,并且她总是为穿衣吃饭育儿操劳,还要成天为那个没有留一文钱买大红肠没丢一个字条做解释就走掉的男人哭泣,他们怎么能不变坏呢?

那些孩子们弄折树木,在汽车中间蹦跳穿梭,膝盖一勾把身体倒挂起来,差点就像博物馆里华美的花瓶一样摔碎了,碎了你就放不回去。他们觉得那很好玩。他们不尊重任何有生命的事物,包括他们自己。

可是不久你就懒得担心了,他们又不是你的孩子。有一天他们在宾尼先生的房顶上玩小鸡。宾尼先生说,嘿你们这些小孩不知道在那里晃悠很危险吗?下来,马上下来。可他们只是啐他。

明白了吧。我说的就是这个。怪不得大家都不管了。小埃弗伦用他的虎牙咬停车计时器的时候,你只要不往外看就可以了;蕾弗佳把头伸进后门上两块板条中间的时候,没人阻止她。那天安琪·法加斯学飞的时候,也没人抬头看一下,她像甜麦圈一样从天上掉下来,就像一颗坠落的流星,砸在地上哦都没哦出一声来。

瞧见老鼠的阿莉西娅

闭上眼,它们就会走掉。她父亲说,也许那只是你的想象。不管怎样,一个女人的本分是睡觉,才能和玉米饼星星[10]一道醒来,那星星现得那样早,早到她起来时,眼角的余光里,能瞥到那些后腿,藏在水槽后面,藏在四脚的盆下面,藏在无人修理的鼓胀地板下面。

阿莉西娅,没了妈妈的她,很难过家里没有一个大过她的人爬起来做装午餐盒的玉米饼。阿莉西娅,继承了妈妈的擀面杖和渴睡的她,年轻聪明,头一次去大学上学,两趟火车和一趟巴士,因为她不想在工厂里,在一根擀面杖后过她的一生。她是个好姑娘,我的朋友,整夜地学习,瞧见老鼠,那些她父亲说不存在的老鼠。她什么都不怕,除了四条腿毛茸茸的东西。还有父亲们[11]。

10 玉米饼星星,指早晨她起来做玉米饼时,在天空中升起的启明星。
11 据作者自述,小时候,她的父亲和六个兄弟都想限制她,企望她成为一个传统的家庭妇女。她说有时感觉自己好像有七个父亲。因此,这里的"父亲们"应该也是指家中的男性。

大流士和云

你永远不能拥有太多的天空。你可以在天空下睡去,醒来又沉醉。在你忧伤的时候,天空会给你安慰。可是忧伤太多,天空不够。蝴蝶也不够,花儿也不够。大多数美的东西都不够。于是,我们取我们所能取,好好地享用。

大流士[12],不喜欢上学的他,有时很傻,几乎是个笨人,今天却说了一句聪明的话,虽然大多数日子他什么都不说。大流士,喜欢用爆竹,用碰过老鼠的小棍子去追逐女孩,还以为自己很了不起的他,今天却指着天空,因为那里有满天的云朵,像枕头样的云朵。

42

你们都看到那朵云了,那朵胖乎乎的云了?大流士说,看到了?哪里?那朵看起来像爆米花的旁边的那朵。那边那朵。看,那是上帝。大流士说。上帝?有个小点的问道。上帝。他说。简洁地说。

12 也是古代波斯帝国国王的名字。一代雄主大流士大帝在位期间(前522—前486),对内强化君主专制,对外实行大规模军事扩张,使得波斯帝国进入全盛期。自命不凡的他曾在贝希斯敦的悬崖上刻下铭文:"我,大流士,伟大的王、万邦之王、波斯之王……我是国王。"后世因此尊他为"万王之王"。

还有……

爱斯基摩人给雪取了三十个不同的名字。我说。我在一本书里读到的。

我有个表妹,拉切尔说,她有三个不同的名字。

世界上没有三十种不同的雪,露西说,只有两种。干净的和脏的,净雪和脏雪。只有两种。

世界上有亿万种雪,蕾妮说,没有两种看上去一模一样。可你怎么记得哪种是哪种?

她有三个名字,让我想想,还有两个姓。一个英语的,一个西班牙语的……

云至少有十个不同的名字。我说。

云的名字?蕾妮问。像你我一样的名字?

那上面那朵,那是积云。每个人都仰起头来看。

积云好可爱呀。拉切尔说。她只会说些这样的话。

那边那朵叫什么?蕾妮问,一个手指指着。

那也是积云。今天全都是积云。积云。积云。积云。

不。她说。那边那朵是南茜,或者叫猪眼。再那边是她的表弟米尔珏德,还有小乔伊、马可、妮雷达和淑儿。

世界上有各种各样的云。你能想起来多少种?

嗯,那边就有一些看上去像剃须泡沫的……

那些看上去像是你用梳子梳过它的毛的呢?是的,那些也是云。

菲力斯、特德、阿尔弗莱德和莱莉……[13]

那边的云看上去像是大片的羊群。拉切尔说,它们我最爱。

别忘了雨云,下雨的云。我说。那也是很重要的云。

何塞、达戈贝尔托、阿莉西娅、劳尔、爱德娜、阿尔玛和里奇……

那边有那种宽宽的胖乎乎的云朵,有点像你没脱衣服就睡着以后醒来的脸。

雷纳尔多、安杰洛、阿尔伯特、阿曼多、马里奥……

不是我的脸。是像你的胖脸。

芮塔、玛吉、爱妮……

是谁的胖脸?

埃斯佩朗莎的胖脸,是她的。像埃斯佩朗莎早上上学去时难看的脸。

爱尼塔、斯妲拉、丹尼斯和萝萝……

你在说谁难看?难看吗?

芮奇、约兰达、赫克托、史蒂夫、文森特……

不是你。是你妈妈。是说她。

我妈妈?你最好别这么说,露西·格莱罗。你最好别这么说话……否则你就永远做不成我的朋友了。

我是说你妈妈难看,就像……嗯……

……像九月的光脚丫!

好吧! 你们两个最好滚出我家院子,别等我叫我弟弟出来。

哦,我们只是说着玩的。

我可以想起三十个爱斯基摩词来说你,拉切尔。三十个骂你的名字。

哦,好,我能想起更多。

嘿,蕾妮。去拿扫帚来。今天我们家院子里垃圾太多了。

弗兰奇、里查、玛利亚、皮威……

蕾妮,你最好告诉你姐姐,她真是疯掉了,露西和我不会再来这里了。永远。

若吉、伊丽莎白、莉莎、路易……

蕾妮,随你做什么,可是如果想做我妹妹的话,最好别和露西或拉切尔讲话。

你知道你是什么吗,埃斯佩朗莎?你就像麦片上的奶油。你就像那些奶泡。

哦,那你就是脚虱,你就是。

小鸡嘴唇。

罗丝玛丽、达丽娅、莉莉……

蟑螂肉。

吉恩、天竺葵和乔……

冰菜豆。

咪咪、迈克尔、莫儿……

你妈妈的菜豆。

你的丑妈妈的脚指头。

蠢呀。

贝贝、布兰卡、宾尼……

谁蠢?

拉切尔、露西、埃斯佩朗莎和蕾妮。

---

13 另外三个小女孩争吵的时候,蕾妮却在自顾自地数云朵,给它们取名字。这里用楷体把她的话标出来,方便理解。

小脚之家

有一家人。都是小个。他们的胳膊很小,他们的手也小,他们的个头也不高,他们的脚非常非常小。

爷爷睡在客厅的沙发上,牙缝里漏出鼾声。他的脚又白又胖,像厚厚的玉米肉粽[14],他把它们扑上粉,套上白袜子,塞进棕色皮靴里。

奶奶的脚像粉红珍珠一样好看,穿着天鹅绒的高跟鞋,走起路来一歪一扭。可她还是穿着它们,因为鞋子漂亮。

宝宝的脚有十个细细的脚趾米,苍白又透明,像蝾螈的脚趾。他只要一饿就会把它们塞进嘴里。

妈妈的脚，丰盈文雅，像白色鸽子从云天，那枕头的海洋飞落，走过油麻毯上的玫瑰，走下木楼梯，走在粉笔画的跳房的格子上，5、6、7，蓝色天空。

你们想要这个吗？给你们个纸袋，里面有一双柠檬黄的鞋子、一双红色的鞋子和一双舞鞋，原先是白色的，现在是淡蓝色的。拿去吧。我们说谢谢你，等到她上楼去。

好哇！今天我们是辛德莱拉[15]，因为我们的脚正合适。我们对着拉切尔一只套着学生灰短袜又穿着女士高跟鞋的脚大笑。你喜欢这些鞋子吗？可说实话，低头看看你的脚，却觉得有点吓人，它好像不再是你的脚了，上面的腿好长好长。

每个人都想换着穿。柠檬黄的换红的，红的换那双曾是白的现在是淡蓝色的。脱下又穿上，穿上又脱下，忙乎了好一阵，直到我们都累了。

然后露西尖声叫起来，我们把袜子脱掉吧。对呀。是真的。我们有腿呀，细瘦的腿，上面点缀着脱痂后形成的缎面疤。可这是我们自己的腿，好看，又长。

拉切尔学会了穿着这些奇妙的高跟鞋，架势十足地走来走去。她教我们把腿交叉又分开，像跳花式绳一样地走；她教我们怎么一步一响地走到街角，好像鞋子在和你对答。

露西、拉切尔和我就这样踮着脚走着。走到街角,男人的眼睛没法从我们身上移开。我们像是带来了圣诞节。

街角杂货店的宾尼先生放下他的大雪茄,问,你们的妈妈知道你们这鞋子哪来的吗?谁给你们的?

没人。

这鞋不安全。他说。你们这些小女孩还太小,不适合穿这样的鞋子。趁我还没叫警察赶快脱掉吧。可我们只是跑开。

大道上一个骑着拼装自行车的男孩喊道,女士们,带我上天堂啊。

那里除了我们没别人。

你喜欢这些鞋子吗?拉切尔说是的,露西说是的,是的,我说,这些是最好的鞋子。我们再也不要穿别的鞋子了。你喜欢这样的鞋子吗?

在自助洗衣店的前面,有六个长着一样的胖脸的女孩,她们装做看不到我们。拉切尔说,他们是表姐妹,喜欢妒忌。我们有模有样地走着。

街对过的一家小酒馆的门前,一个流浪汉坐在长凳上。

你喜欢这鞋子吗?

流浪汉说,喜欢,小姑娘。你的小黄鞋好漂亮。走近点,我看不太清。再近点。来。

你是漂亮的小姑娘,那个人接着说,你叫什么名字,美女?

拉切尔说叫拉切尔。就那么答了一句。

现在你知道和醉鬼说话有多不好了吧,告诉他你的名字就更糟糕,可谁能怪她呢。她那么小,一天里听到那么多好听的话让她有点晕头了,即便那是一个流浪汉的醉话。

拉切尔,你比一辆黄色出租车还漂亮。你知道吗?

可我们不喜欢。我们得走了。露西说。

如果我给你一元钱你会吻我吗?一元钱怎么样?我给你一元钱,他低头在口袋里找起皱巴巴的票子来。

我们得马上走,露西说着拉过拉切尔的手,因为她好像在考虑那一元钱呢。

流浪汉冲着空气在叫喊着什么,可我们已经很快地跑远了,我们的高跟鞋带着我们一路跑过大街,转过街区,经过那一群难看的表姐妹,经过宾尼先生的店,跑到了芒果街上,回来了,以防万一。

我们厌倦了扮靓。露西把柠檬黄的、红色的和先是白色后来是淡蓝色的鞋子藏在后廊上一个很大的篮子里,直到星期二,她妈妈,非常爱干净的她,把它们扔了。没有人抗议。

---

14 Tamale,一种墨西哥著名食品,由玉米、碎肉和辣椒裹在一起蒸制而成。
15 Cinderella,格林童话中穿水晶鞋的灰姑娘的名字。

✳饭三明治

那些特殊的孩子,那些脖子上套着钥匙的孩子,他们在餐厅吃饭。餐厅![16] 名字听起来就不一样。那些孩子在午餐时间去那里,因为他们的妈妈不在家,或者家太远了不好回。

我的家不远,也不近。有一天我不知怎么想起来要妈妈帮我做一个三明治,并写上一张纸条给校长,那样我就也可以在餐厅吃饭了。

哦,不,她用切黄油的小刀指着我,好像我正在挑起事端一样。不行,长官。你知道接下来的事情就是每个人都会想带盒饭——我夜里就得忙着把面包切成三角丁,这个抹上蛋黄酱,那个撒上胡椒,我的不要泡菜,每面都要胡椒末。你们这些孩子就喜欢给我找事儿。

可蕾妮说她从不想在学校吃,因为她喜欢和她最要好的朋友一起回家,格洛莉亚住在校园对面。格洛莉亚的妈妈有个大彩电,她们就在那里看卡通片。另外,奇奇和卡洛斯是童子军,他们也不想在学校吃。他们喜欢站在寒冷中,尤其在下雨的时候。自从看了电影《斯巴达三百壮》[17]后,他们就认为吃苦有好处。

我可不是斯巴达人。我伸出一只苍白的手腕来证明。不吹到头晕的话我就吹不爆一个气球。还有,我知道怎么给自己准备午餐。如果我在学校吃,你就可以少洗几个盘子。你看到我的时间少了就会更喜欢我。每天中午我的椅子是空的。你会哭着说我那心爱的丫头呢。而最后我三点钟回家的时候,你会更欣赏我。

好的。好的。妈妈在我这样磨了她三天后说。第二天早上我上学的时候就带着妈妈的信和一个米饭三明治,因为我们午饭没肉吃。

是星期一还是星期五?这不重要。早晨总是过去很慢,那天尤其是。午餐时间终于到了,我得和留校的孩子们一起排队。一切都很顺利,直到那个记得所有在餐厅吃饭的小孩的嬷嬷看着我说,你,谁让你来这里的?我因为害羞,什么都没说,只是伸出拿着信的手。这样不好,她说,得大嬷嬷说好才行。上楼去见她吧。于是我就走上楼。

我得等两个在我前面的小孩进去听训,他们一个是因为上课时干了什么事情,一个是因为上课时没干什么事情。轮到我了,我站在那张大桌子前面,桌子的玻璃板下面压着一幅圣像。大嬷嬷读着我的信。信是这样写的:

亲爱的大嬷嬷:

请让埃斯佩朗莎在午餐厅吃饭,因为她住得很远,会走累的。你看她有多瘦啊。上帝保佑她不会晕倒。

谢谢。

E.科尔德罗太太

你住得不远,她说。你住在大街对面。只有四个街区。甚至还没有。也许是三个。离这里只有三个街区。我肯定我能从窗户里看到你家。哪一栋?来这边。哪栋是你家?

接着她让我站在一盒子书上面去指给她看。那栋吗？她说，指着一排丑陋的三户式公寓楼，那里是衣衫褴褛的人都羞于走进去的地方。是的，我点头，尽管我知道那里不是我家。我哭了起来。我经常在嬷嬷朝我吼的时候哭，尽管她们没有吼。

然后她很抱歉，说我可以留下来，只是今天，明天或者以后——你就回家。我说好的，可以给我一张面纸[18]吗？——我要擤擤鼻子。

到了餐厅，那里没什么特别的。好多男孩和女孩看着我边哭边吃三明治，那面包已经很油腻了。米饭也冷掉了。

---

16 原文是 Canteen，来自法文的英文单词，小孩听来可能觉得洋气。
17 一部经典战争片。讲述公元前 480 年波斯人入侵希腊，斯巴达国王列奥尼达斯率领三百壮士对抗压境强敌，在力量对比极为悬殊的情况下，以少抗多，血战至死，宣扬了一种无畏的英雄主义气概。斯巴达是一个军事社会，所有男子未等成年都要接受艰苦的军事训练，来锻炼他们的意志和作战能力。
18 原文是 Kleenex，是世界上最早的面纸品牌，因此，很多美国人保持了把面纸叫成"kleenex"的习惯。Kleenex 品牌到了中国就是"舒洁牌"。

塌跟的旧鞋 [19]

是我——妈妈。妈妈说。我开了门，她站在那里拎着大盒小包，是新衣服，是的，她买了袜子、一件上面有朵玫瑰花的背带裙和一件粉红条间白条的裙子。鞋子呢？我忘了。现在太晚了，我好累哟。唉。

已经六点半了。我小表弟的洗礼式已经过了。一天都在等待，门锁着。没人来别开门。我没开，直到妈妈回来，什么都买回来了，就忘了鞋子。

现在拿乔叔叔开着车来了。我们得赶去圣血[20]教堂，因为洗礼晚会在那里举行。他们今天租了那里的地下室用来跳舞和吃玉米肉粽。家家户户的孩子满地乱跑。

妈妈跳呀笑呀又跳。忽然,她不舒服了。我用一个纸碟对着她滚烫的脸扇风。玉米肉粽太多了,可拿乔叔叔这句话也说太多遍了,他用拇指按了按嘴唇。

每个人都在笑,除了我,因为我穿着粉红条间白条的新裙子、新内衣和新袜子,却套了双旧凉鞋,那是穿去学校的鞋子,棕色间白色的,那种我每年九月就会得到的鞋子,因为它很耐用,实在耐用。鞋面都磨圆了,鞋跟也歪了,配身上的衣服显得好笨。于是我只好坐在那里。

这时那个男孩来请我跳舞,可我不能。他是我的一个表哥,在第一次圣餐会[21]还是什么时候认识的。我只是把脚缩在贴有圣血教堂标签的金属折叠椅下面,还从椅子下面摘到一粒黏在上面的褐色香口胶。我摇头说不。我的脚好像越来越大了。

拿乔叔叔拉呀拉我的胳膊,妈妈买的衣服多新都没用,只是我的脚太难看了,直到我那个撒谎者叔叔说,你是这里最漂亮的姑娘,你能跳支舞吗?不过我相信他的话,是的,我们跳了起来,我的拿乔叔叔和我,我只是开始不想跳。我的脚肿了,老大老沉,像铅垂一样。可我拖着它们走过油麻毯到了正中央,拿乔叔叔想在那里炫一下我们新学会的舞蹈。叔叔转动着我,我细长的胳膊照他教的那样弯曲着,妈妈在看,小表弟在看,那个我第一次圣餐会认识的表哥也在看,大家都说,这两个人怎么跳得像电影里的一样啊。跳到后来,我忘记了自己穿的只是很平常的鞋子,棕色间白色的,那种妈妈每年买了给我上学的鞋子。

音乐停下来时,我听到的都是掌声。叔叔和我一起鞠了一躬,然后他护送穿着厚鞋子的我走回到妈妈身边,妈妈为她是我的妈妈而骄傲。整个夜晚,那个是男人的男孩都在看我跳舞。他看我跳舞。

19　原文为 chanclas,西班牙语,意为"塌跟的旧鞋"。
20　Precious Blood,指基督被钉在十字架上时流的血,可洗净世人的罪。
21　天主教的一种仪式,是父母为迎接自己的孩子进入教会,进入教徒的家庭而举行的一次亲朋好友的聚会。

髋骨

我喜欢咖啡,我喜欢茶。

我喜欢男孩呀男孩也喜欢我。

是也不是也许是。是也不是也许是……

某一天,你醒过来,它们就在那里了。一切就绪,等在那里,像一辆崭新的别克[22],钥匙插在点火器上。一切就绪带你去哪里呢?

拉切尔说,你做饭的时候,它们可以帮你托住孩子,说着便把跳绳晃得更快了。她一点想象力都没有。

你需要用它们来跳舞。露西说。

如果你没有它们,就会变成男人。蕾妮这么说,她也是这么以为的。她这样是因为她的年龄。

是的。没等拉切尔和露西笑话她,我就接着说。她是很笨,可她是我妹妹。

最重要的是,髋骨是很科学的。我重复着阿莉西娅告诉过我的话。凭着这两块骨头你可以知道一架骷髅是女人的还是男人的。

它们像玫瑰一样绽放,我接着说。显然,我是这里唯一讲话有说服力的人。我有科学的支撑。有一天那两块骨头会张开。像这样张开。有一天你也许会决定要孩子,可是把它们放哪里呢?得有空位置。骨头会给出空位置。

不过别要太多的孩子,否则你的后背会张得很宽的。后背就是那么变宽的。拉切尔说。她妈妈宽得像条船。我们都笑起来。

我想要说的是,这里谁准备好了呢?你们得知道,长了髋骨之后该怎么对它,照我的样子来做吧,你们得知道怎么用髋骨走路,你们知道的,这样练习——好像你身体的一半想往这边走,另一半却想往那边走。

这是在给它唱摇篮曲呢,蕾妮说,是在摇你身体里面的宝宝入睡。接着她就唱开了:海螺房呀铜铃铛,伊薇在那常青藤上晃呀。

我想告诉她这是我听到过的最傻的歌,可是我越琢磨它越……

你得押韵。露西开始跳起舞来。她有想法,虽然她不知道怎么把她那端的荷兰绳晃得均匀。

要正正好才行。我说。不要太快也不要太慢。别太快也别太慢。

我们把双圈降到一定的速度,好让刚跳进去的拉切尔先练习几下摇晃的动作。

我想像呼哧库哧那样摇。露西说。她真是来劲。

我想像希比吉比 [23] 一样晃,我学她的样儿说。

我想做塔希提 [24] 人。还有默朗格 [25] 人。还有电。

或者震簪 [26]!

对,震簪。这个好。

然后拉切尔先唱了起来:

蹦一蹦,跳一跳,

屁股摇一摇。

水蛇儿扭上来,

嘴唇呀被钻开。

轮到露西的时候,她等了一分钟,想了想,然后唱道:

女招待呀长着肥肥屁股,

她用那的士小费付她的房租……

她说这城里没人吻她的唇部

因为……

因为她长得像克里斯托弗·哥伦布!

是也不是也许是,是也不是也许是。

她唱到"也许是"时跳空了。轮到我之前,我想了一会,然后吸了口气,跳了进去:

有的像小鸡嘴儿干瘪瘪,

有的像邦迪贴儿湿鼓鼓,

只要你一把澡盆儿出,

只要我长呀长出屁股来
不管不管它是瘪还是鼓。

　　每个人都参加进来了,除了蕾妮,她还在哼着不是女孩,不是男孩,只是一个小宝宝。她就像个小宝宝。当两条绳子的弧度像上下颌一样分得很开时,蕾妮从我眼前跳了进去。绳子啪嗒啪嗒地晃动,妈妈在她第一次圣餐会的时候给她的金耳坠也在晃动。她的颜色就像一块轻油洗衣皂,她就像洗到最后剩下那棕色的一小块,坚硬的小皂骨,我的妹妹。她张开嘴,开始唱道:

我妈妈呀你妈妈都在洗衣裳,
我妈妈拳头捶在你妈妈鼻子上,
流出来的血是呀是什么颜色?

　　不是那首老歌。我说。你得唱你自己的歌。自己编,知道吗?可她没弄明白,或者不想弄明白。很难说到底是哪种原因。绳子摇呀摇呀摇。

> 机车机车第九号,
> 芝城铁路线上跑。
> 如果火车把轨抛,
> 你可会想退了票
> 你可会想把钱要。
> 是也不是也许是,是也不是也许是……

我可以看出来露西和拉切尔有点气愤。可她们没说什么,因为她是我妹妹。

> 是也不是也许是。是也不是也许是……

蕾妮。我喊她。可她没听到我。她远在好多光年外。她在一个我们再也不属于的世界里。蕾妮。走呀,走呀。

> Y—E—S,拼好 Y—E—S 你就走!

22　美国的小汽车品牌,特点是车身宽阔,行驶过程中后身会微微摇摆。

23 Hoochie Coochie，上世纪六十年代中期流行的一支布鲁斯乐队，其主打歌曲 *Hoochie Coochie Men* 是广泛流传的布鲁斯经典曲目。Heebie Jeebies，摇滚乐队名。heebie-jeebie，俚语，指起鸡皮疙瘩，或头皮发麻的感觉。这两支乐队演唱时，伴唱动作常呈摇摆或颤抖状。

24 对居住在南太平洋波利尼西亚群岛中的塔希提岛上的土著人来说，歌舞是他们最重要的交流方式，他们的舞蹈热情而富于表现力，激发许多艺术大师创作出杰作，如高更的塔希提系列和马蒂斯的《音乐》。

25 Merengue，一种发源于海地的欢快而优美的舞蹈，为多米尼加共和国的国舞。

26 Tembleque，西班牙语，震簪，即用细金属丝吊着的、不停震颤的珠宝簪子。

第一份工

我才不是不想工作呢。我想的。甚至,我上个月已经去社会安全司拿了我的社会安全号。我需要钱。天主教会高中收费很高,爸爸说没人会去公立学校,除非你想变坏。

我想我会找到一个轻松的工作,那种和别的小孩干的一样的,在一个零售小店或者热狗摊上打工。虽然还没开始找,我想我下下个星期就会找到的。那天下午我回家时,全身都湿透了,因为提陀把我推进了敞口的消防水栓里——是我自己惹得他这么做的——还没来得及换衣服,妈妈就把我叫进了厨房,娜拉阿姨坐在那里用小勺喝咖啡。娜拉阿姨说,她在她工作的北百老汇大道上的彼得·潘照片冲印店里帮我找了份工。又问我多大,说明天去的时候要把自己说大一岁,如此这般。

于是第二天我穿上那件让我看上去显大的海军蓝的裙子,又借了午餐和公交车钱,因为娜拉阿姨说要到下个星期五我才能拿到钱。然后,我就进去了,见到了娜拉阿姨工作的北百老汇大道上的彼得·潘照片冲印店的老板,照她说的谎报了年龄,果然,我从那天就开始干了。

我做事时要戴上白手套。他们让我做的是把底片和相片配好,就是对着相片在底片条上找到那张的底片,把它放进信封里,然后再配下一张。就这些。我不知道那些信封从哪里来,要到哪里去。我只是按吩咐的去做。

真的好容易。我想我本来不会介意的,可干了一会我有点累,不知道是否可以坐,于是就看着旁边的两位女士,她们坐下来的时候我才坐。过了一会她们笑起来,走过来跟我说可以想坐就坐的,我说我知道。

午餐时间到了,我不敢一个人跑到有那么多先生和女士们看着你的公司餐厅里去吃,就站在一间盥洗室里很快地吃完了,结果剩下很多时间,就早早地回去干活了。然后又到了休息时间,不知道去哪里好,我就走进了衣帽间,因为那里有条长凳。

我想那时是上晚班或者中班的人来接班的时候,因为有几个人进来打卡。一个上了年纪的东方人跟我打招呼,我们聊了一会我刚开始上班的事情,他说我们会成为朋友,下次去餐厅可以和他坐一起。我感觉好点了。他的眼睛很和善,我没那么紧张了。接着他问我,知道今天是什么日子吗?我说我不知道。他就说是他的生日,问我愿不愿意给他一个生日吻。我想我愿意,因为他很老了,正在我想要把嘴唇贴到他脸颊上时,他双手捧过我的脸,重重地亲我的嘴,不放开。

黑暗里醒来的疲惫的爸爸

你爷爷去世了。有天清晨很早的时候,爸爸到我房里来说。他不在了[27],说完,他好像自己才听到这个消息一样,人像件外套一样皱缩起来,哭了。我勇敢的爸爸哭了。我从来没看过爸爸哭,不知道该怎么办。

我知道他要走了,他会坐飞机去墨西哥,所有的叔叔婶婶都会去那里。他们会拍上一张黑白照片,在摆着白色花瓶的墓地边,花瓶里插着长矛状的花束。在那个国家里,人们就那样送别死者。

因为我是最大的孩子,爸爸最先和我说起,现在轮到我来告诉别的人。我会解释为什么我们不能玩耍。我会告诉他们今天要安静。

我的爸爸,厚厚的手掌沉沉的鞋,黑暗里疲惫地起身,蘸水梳头,喝掉咖啡,平日在我们醒来之前就走了的爸爸,今天正坐在我的床边。

我想要是我自己的爸爸死去了我会做什么。于是我把爸爸抱在怀里,我要抱啊抱啊抱住他。

---

27 此处原文为西班牙文,是对前面一句话意思的重复,渲染出悲伤的氛围。

生辰不吉

很可能我会去地狱,很可能我该去那里。妈妈说我出生的日子不吉利,并为我祈祷。露西和拉切尔也祈祷。为我们自己也为相互之间……为我们对卢佩婶婶做的事情。

她的全名叫瓜达卢佩[28]。她像我妈妈一样漂亮。暗色皮肤。十分耐看。穿着琼·克劳馥式的裙子,长着游泳者的腿。那是照片上的卢佩婶婶。

可我知道她生病了,疾病缠绵不去。她的腿绑束在黄色的床单下面,骨头变得和蠕虫一样软弱。黄色的枕头,黄色的气味,瓶子勺子。她像一个口渴的女人一样向后仰着头。

我的婶婶,那个游泳者。

很难想象她的腿曾经强健。坚韧的骨,劈波分浪,动作干净爽利,没有像婴儿的腿那样蜷曲皱缩,也没有淹滞在黏浊的黄光灯下。二层楼背面的公寓。光秃的电灯泡。高高的天花板,灯泡一直在燃烧。

我不知道是谁来决定谁该遭受厄运。她出生的日子没有不吉利。没有邪恶的诅咒。头一天我想她还在游泳,第二天她就病了。可能是拍下那张灰色照片的那天。也可能是她抱着表弟托奇和宝宝弗兰克的那天。也可能是她指着照相机让小孩们看可他们不看的那一刻。

也许天空在她摔倒的那天没有看向人间。也许上帝很忙。也许那天她入水没入好伤了脊椎是真的,也许托奇说的是真的,她从高高的梯凳上重重地摔了下来。

我想疾病没有眼睛。它们昏乱的指头会挑到任何人,任何人。比如我的婶婶,那天正好走在街上的婶婶,穿着琼·克劳馥式裙子,戴着缀有黑羽毛的、滑稽的毡帽,一只手里是表弟托奇,一只手里是宝宝弗兰克。

有时你会习惯病人,有时你会习惯疾病,如果病得太久,也就习以为常了。她的情况就是这样。或者这就是我们选择她的原因。

那是一个游戏。仅此而已。我们每天下午都玩的游戏,自从某天我们中的一个发明了它。我不记得是谁,我想那是我。

你得挑选一个人。你得想出大家都知道的一个人,一个你可以模仿,而别人都能猜出来的人。先是那些名人:神奇女侠[29]、披头士、玛丽莲·梦露……后来有人认为我们稍稍改变一下,如果我们假装自己是宾尼先生,或者他的妻子布兰卡,或者鹭鸶儿,或者别的我们认识的人,游戏会好玩点。

我不知道我们为什么挑选了她。也许那天我们很无聊,也许我们累了。我们喜欢我们的婶婶。她会听我们讲故事。她经常求我们再来。露西、我和拉切尔。我讨厌一个人去那里。走六个街区才到那昏暗的公寓,阳光从不会照射到的二层楼背面的房子,可那有什么关系?我婶婶那时已经瞎了。她从来看不见水池里的脏碗碟。她看不到落满灰尘和苍蝇的天花板。难看的酱色墙壁,瓶瓶罐罐和黏腻的茶勺。我无法忘记那里的气味。就像黏黏的胶囊注满了冻糊糊。我婶婶,一瓣小牡蛎,一团小肉,躺在打开的壳上,供我们观看。喂,喂。她好像掉在一口深井里。

我把从图书馆借的书带到她家里。我给她读故事。我喜欢《水孩子》[30]这本书。她也喜欢。我从来不知道她病得有多重,直到那天我想要指给她看书里的一幅画,美丽的画,水孩子在大海中游泳。我把书举到她眼前。我看不到。她说。我瞎了。我心里便很愧疚。

她会听我念给她听的每一本书,每一首诗。一天我读了一首自己写的给她听。我凑得很近。我对着枕头轻轻耳语:

> 我想成为
> 海里的浪,风中的云,
> 但我还只是小小的我。
> 有一天我要
> 跳出自己的身躯,
> 我要摇晃天空,
> 像一百把小提琴。

很好。非常好。她用有气无力的声音说。记住你要写下去,埃斯佩朗莎。你一定要写下去。那会让你自由,我说好的,只是那时我还不懂她的意思。

那天我们玩了同样的游戏。我们不知道她要死了。我们装做头往后仰，四肢软弱无力，像死人的一样垂挂着。我们学她的样子笑。学她的样子说话，那种盲人说话的时候不转动头部的样子。我们模仿她必须被人托起头颈才能喝水的样子。她从一个绿色的锡杯里把水慢慢地吮出来喝掉。水是热的，味道像金属。露西笑起来，拉切尔也笑了。我们轮流扮演她。我们像鹦鹉学舌一样，用微弱的声音呼喊托奇过来洗碗。那很容易做到。

可我们不懂。她等待死亡很长时间了。我们忘了。也许她很愧疚。也许她很窘迫：死亡花了这么多年时间。孩子们想要当回孩子，而不是在那里洗碗涮碟，给爸爸熨衬衫。丈夫也想再要一个妻子。

于是她死了。听我念诗的婶婶。

于是我们开始做起了那些梦。

28　Guadalupe，也是墨西哥圣母的名字。每年12月12日的瓜达卢佩圣母节（Guadalupe Day）是墨西哥最重要的宗教节日。
29　上世纪七十年代非常流行的一部由漫画改编的电影《神奇女侠》中的主人公，是美国漫画史上第一位漫画女英雄。

30 《水孩子》(*The Water Babies*),查理·金斯莱(1819—1875)的一部童话经典,讲述小烟囱工汤姆在仙女的帮助下,逃离危险的苦役,去到一处安宁清洁的水下世界,做了个水孩子。后来,经过一连串的奇遇,他习得了各种美德,完成了自己的成长之路,回到陆地,成为一个仁爱正直的人。国内早有周煦良的译本。作者金斯莱是牛津、剑桥的历史学教授,还曾做过维多利亚女王的牧师。学识渊博的他,写出的童话却清新优美,寄寓着对所有稚嫩心灵的爱惜与期望。

伊伦妮塔、牌、手掌和水

伊伦妮塔,算命的女人,用抹布擦桌子,因为喂宝宝的埃妮把酷爱汁[31]洒了。她说,把这蠢宝宝抱出去,到客厅里去喝你的酷爱。你没看到我在忙吗?埃妮把宝宝抱去了客厅,那里的电视上在演《兔八哥》[32]。

幸亏你昨天没来,她说,昨天星星全乱套了。

她的电视是彩色的,很大,她所有漂亮的家具都是用嘉年华会上派送的泰迪熊那样的红色毛皮做的。她在上面蒙了一层塑料。我想这都是因为宝宝的缘故。

是的,那是好事情。我说。

我们待在厨房里,因为这里是她工作的地方。冰柜的顶上摆满了东西:点着和没点着的圣烛,有红有绿有蓝;一个石膏圣像和一个灰扑扑的棕榈主日十字架,一张用胶带贴在墙上的伏都[33]神手图。

去弄点水来。她说。

我走到水池边拿起那里唯一干净的杯子,一个大啤酒杯,上面写着"啤酒使密尔瓦齐[34]闻名于世"。我用它从水龙头里接了点热水,然后把这杯水放到了桌子中央,这是她教我的。

看里面,看到什么了吗?

可我看到的只是气泡。

你看到谁的脸了吗?

没有,只有泡泡。我说。

好吧。她用手在水面上画了三次十字,开始抽牌。

这可不是平常玩的牌。这些牌,[35]它们有点奇怪,上面有骑在马上的金发白肤的男人、吓人的长了刺的棒球棒、金色圣杯、穿着旧式服装的悲伤的女人,还有哭泣的玫瑰。

我知道电视上在演一部好玩的《兔八哥》卡通片。我以前看过,听出了它的音乐,我希望可以走过去和埃妮、宝宝一起坐在塑料沙发上,可我的命运开始显现了。我的一生都在这厨房桌子上:过去、现在和将来。接着她拿起我的手看手掌。合上它。同时合上的还有她的眼睛。

你感觉到了吗?感觉到冷了吗?

是的,我撒谎说,有一点冷。

好。她说,精灵[36]在里面。开始了。

这张牌,上面有一个黑人骑黑马的,代表嫉妒;这张,代表忧伤。这里有一窝蜜蜂和一张豪华床垫。你马上要去参加一个婚礼了。你丢失了一双可以依靠的臂膀是吗?对,可靠的臂膀?很清楚,这就是它代表的意思。

有房子吗?我问,我是因为它才来的。

啊,是的,心中有一所房子。我在心中看到一所房子。

那是房子吗?

我看到的是的。她说着便站起来,因为孩子们在打架。伊伦妮塔站起来打了他们,然后又抱抱他们。她很爱他们,只是他们有时太野了。

她回来,能看出来我有些失望。她是个算命的女人,知道很多事情。如果你头痛,就把一个冷鸡蛋抹在脸上。要忘掉一桩过去的恋情是吗?拿一只小鸡爪,系上红绳子,在你脑袋上旋转三次,然后烧掉它。恶幽灵让你睡不着是吗?靠近一支圣烛睡七天,到第八天的时候,点燃它。还有好多好多其他的事情。而现在她知道我有点伤心。

宝贝,如果你想的话,我可以再看一次。于是她又看了一遍牌、手掌、水。啊哈。她说。

心里的一所房子,我是对的。

可我还是不明白。

一所新房子,一所心造的房子。我会为你点上一支烛。

我为这个付了她五元钱。

谢谢,再见。当心罪恶之眼。等星期三星星再强一点的时候再来。圣母保佑你。门关上了。

---

31 Kool-aid,一种软饮料品牌。此处是音译译名。
32 Bugs Bunny,华纳动画片中的著名的卡通兔形象。
33 Voodoo,一种发源于西非的古老而神秘的原始宗教,又作巫毒教。Voodoo 一词源自西非芳族人(Fon)的语言,意为"灵魂"。伏都教伴随向美洲的移民传入中美洲,结合了印第安人原始宗教的特点,又融入了一些天主教的仪式。伏都教尤盛于海地。

34 Milwaukee,密尔瓦齐,美国威斯康星州东南部城市,其啤酒厂久负盛名。
35 这里的牌是塔罗牌(tarot),一种古老的占卜工具,由22张大阿尔克纳牌(major arcana)和56张小阿尔克纳牌(minor arcana)组成。从代表流浪的零号愚人牌到代表达成的二十一号世界牌,每张大阿尔克纳牌上都绘有不同的神秘画面。在占卜中,这些画面的寓意被用来解释未来和命运。
36 此处为西班牙语。

没有姓的杰拉尔多

她在一次舞会上遇到他。也挺漂亮的,年轻。说他在一家餐馆工作,可她不记得是哪一家。杰拉尔多。就这些。绿色的裤子,星期六的衬衫。杰拉尔多。他告诉她的就这些。

她怎么会知道她是最后一个见到他活着的人呢?一场事故,你不明白吗?司机撞了人就跑掉了。玛琳,各种各样的舞会她都去。上城。摇石。使馆。帕尔默。阿拉贡。喷泉。庄园。她喜欢跳舞。她知道怎么跳昆比亚、萨尔萨,甚至还有兰切拉[37]而他只是一个和她跳舞的人。一个她那晚的偶遇。是这样的。

事情就是这样。她说了一遍又一遍。一次对医院里的人,两次对警察。没有地址。没有姓名。口袋里什么都没有。倒霉吧。

只是玛琳无法解释自己为什么会在意,对一个她甚至不认识的人,一个小时又一个小时过去了。医院的急救室。除了一个实习生在那里忙,没有人来。如果他没失那么多血,也许外科医生会来,如果外科医生来了,他们会知道去通知谁通知哪里。

可这有什么不一样呢?他又不是她什么人。他不是她的男朋友或类似男朋友的人。只是又一个不会讲英语的墨西哥苦力[38]。又一个偷渡客[39]。你知道那些人。看上去总是自惭形秽的人。可凌晨三点她在那里做什么呢?和她的外套以及一些阿司匹林一起被送回家的玛琳,她怎么解释呢?

她在一次舞会上遇到他。穿着绿色裤子和闪亮衬衫的杰拉尔多。参加舞会的杰拉尔多。

可这有什么关系呢?

他们从未见过那个小厨房。他们从不知道他租的那套两室公寓和几间睡房。每周寄回家里的薪水汇票,还有兑换的货币。他们怎么知道呢?

他的名字叫杰拉尔多。他的家在另外一个国家。他留在身后的人在远方,他们会奇怪,耸耸肩,又想起来。杰拉尔多,他去了北面……我们再也没收到过他的信了。

37 昆比亚、萨尔萨和兰切拉是三种深受拉美人民喜爱的音乐。昆比亚是哥伦比亚的国乐,热烈欢快。萨尔萨由古巴颂乐演化而来,自由奔放。兰切拉是墨西哥的乡村歌曲,歌词简单,朴素自然。
38 Brazer,指上世纪来到美国,包揽那些懒惰的白人不愿做的重活的墨西哥人。
39 Wetback,墨西哥裔移民,尤指非法入境的一类。曾经,偷渡的墨西哥人经常游泳过河进入美国,上岸时背上是湿的,这个单词即由此而来。

埃德娜的鹭鸶儿

鹭鸶儿,细高个的瘦骨美人,涂着红红的唇膏,绑着蓝色的阿婆头巾,因为疏忽了而穿着一只蓝袜和一只绿袜的她,是我们认识的唯一喜欢玩的大人。她带着她的狗波波散步,一个人大声笑。那个鹭鸶儿。她不需要别人陪她一起笑。她就那么笑。

她是埃德娜的女儿,拥有隔壁那所大房子的女人,前后加起来有三套公寓。每个星期埃德娜都会冲着某个人尖叫,每个星期都有人得搬走。有一次她赶出去一个怀孕的女人,只因为她养了只小鸭……那可是只漂亮的小鸭。可鹭鸶儿住在这里,埃德娜不能赶走她,因为鹭鸶儿是她的女儿。

鹭鸶儿是有一天忽然来到的,像是不知从哪里冒出来的。安琪·法加斯正在教我们怎么吹口哨。然后我们就听到有人在吹——美妙得像皇帝的夜莺——我们回头的时候,鹭鸶儿就在那里了。

有时我们去逛街就带上她。可她从来不进店里去。如果她进了店,就会不停地四下张望,好像一头第一次被关进屋子里的野生动物。

她喜欢糖。我们去宾尼先生的杂货店时,她会给我们钱帮她带一些。她说要看清是那种软糖再买,因为她的牙齿疼。然后她答应下星期去看牙医,可下星期到了,她也没去。

鹭鸶儿能在每一处看见美丽的事物。有时我正在跟她讲一个笑话,她会停下来说:月亮多美呀像个气球。或者有人在唱歌时,她会指着几朵云彩说:看,马龙·白兰度。或者一个眨眼睛的斯芬克司女妖。或者我左脚的鞋子。

有一次埃德娜的几个朋友过来拜访,问鹭鸶儿愿不愿意和他们去玩宾戈牌。汽车发动机嗡嗡响着,鹭鸶儿站在楼梯上想要不要去。我应该去吗,妈?她对着二楼纱窗后面那个灰色的影子发问。我不管,纱窗说,你想去就去。鹭鸶儿看着地面。你怎么认为,妈?做你想做的,我怎么知道?鹭鸶儿又看了看地面。开着发动机的汽车等了十五分钟,然后他们走了。那晚我们拿出那副纸牌来时,我们让鹭鸶儿发牌。

如果她想的话,鹭鸶儿本来可以成为很多种人的。这不仅是因为她口哨吹得好,她还很会唱歌和跳舞。她年轻的时候有很多工作机会,可她从来没做过。她结婚了,搬进了城外一所漂亮的大房子里。我弄不明白的一件事情就是,为什么鹭鸶儿住在芒果街上,她本来可以不住的;为什么她有自己的真正的大房子却要睡在她妈妈的客厅沙发上? 她说她只是来看看,下周末她丈夫会来接她回家。可周末来了又去了,鹭鸶儿还在这里。这没什么。我们很高兴,因为她是我们的朋友。

我喜欢给她看我从图书馆带出来的书。书很棒,鹭鸶儿说,然后就用手抚摩起来,似乎她可以像读布莱叶盲文一样地读它们。很棒,很棒,可我再也不能读书了。我头痛。我下星期得去看眼科医生。我过去写过童书的,我告诉过你吗?

一天我把"海象和木匠"[40]全都背了下来,因为我想让鹭鸶儿听听。"日光光,耀海洋;光芒万里长……"鹭鸶儿看着天空,好几次她的眼睛变湿了。我终于背到了最后几行:

"无人应一嗓,此事不荒唐:可怜小牡蛎,个个被吃光……"她看着我,久久不开口。最后她说,你有着我见过的最漂亮的牙齿,然后便走到里面去了。

---

40 《爱丽丝镜中奇遇记》里的一首长诗。叙述一群年幼无知的小牡蛎在海象和木匠的诱骗下爬上海滩,最后塞了他们牙缝的故事。

田纳西的埃尔 [41]

埃尔住在隔壁埃德娜家的地下室里,在埃德娜每年都要漆成绿色的花箱后面,在那些灰蒙蒙的天竺葵后面。我们以前常坐在花箱上,直到有一天,提陀看到一只脑袋上有一点绿漆的蟑螂。现在我们坐在拐向埃尔住的地下室的楼梯台阶上。

埃尔上夜班。他的百叶窗在白天总是合上的。有时他会出来叫我们保持安静。已经开裂的小木门把黑暗关在里面那么久,现在它打开了,呀的一声叹息,吐出一口潮湿的霉气,就像放在外面淋过雨的书。这是唯一一次我们不是在他回来和去上班的时候看到他。他有两条与他形影不离的小黑犬。它们不是像平常的狗那么走路,而是一蹦一跳,翻着筋斗前进,像一个撇号和一个逗号。

夜里,蕾妮和我能听到埃尔下班回家的声音。先是汽车门打开时的喀哒声和低鸣,接着是走过水泥地的嚓嚓脚步声、小狗身上坠饰兴奋的丁零声,跟着是钥匙沉重的当啷声。最后是木门开启吐出湿气时的呻吟声。

埃尔是一个自动唱机修理工。他在南边的时候学了这门手艺。他说。他说话带南方口音,抽粗肥的雪茄,戴一顶毡帽,无论冬夏炎凉,都是这一顶。在他的寓所里是一盒一盒的 45 转唱片,潮湿发霉,像他每次开门时寓所里出来的气味一样。他把唱片全都送给我们,除了乡村和西部的。

据说埃尔结婚了,在哪里有个妻子。埃德娜说埃尔带她回公寓的时候她见过她一次。妈妈说她是个细瘦的人,金发淡肤,苍白得像从未见过阳光的蝾螈。可我也见过她一次,根本不是那样的。街对面的男孩说她是一个高个红发女郎,穿粉红紧身裤,戴绿眼镜。我们从来没在她的长相上达成一致,可我们确实知道这事。她每次来,他都紧紧握着她的胳膊肘。他们飞快地走进寓所,在身后锁上门,从来不久待。

---

41 田纳西,美国东南部一州,埃尔是从那里来的人。

塞尔

我不记得什么时候起,发觉他在看我,塞尔。可我知道他在看。每次,我从他家房前走过时,他一直在看。他和他的朋友在房子前,坐在自行车上抛硬币。他们没吓我。他们吓着我了,可我不会让他们知道。我不像别的女孩那样过街。我走了过去,笔直向前,笔直的视线。我知道他在看。我要向自己证明,我不害怕任何人的眼睛,即便是他的。我要回头用力看,就一眼,当他是块玻璃。于是我那么做了。我看了一眼,可我看得太久,在他骑过我身边的时候,我看是因为我想勇敢些,一直看到他眼睛上灰蒙蒙的猫毛里去。自行车停下来，撞在一辆停着的小汽车上，撞到了，我于是飞快地走开。有人那样看你会让你的血结冰。有人看我。有人看。可是他是那样的人，他那样看。他是个小混混。爸爸说。别和他说话。妈妈说。

后来他女朋友来了。我听到他叫她罗伊丝。她又美又娇小，散发出婴儿皮肤的味道。我见她有时去商店为他买东西。有次在宾尼先生的店里，她站在我身旁。她光着脚，我看到那光脚丫上婴儿一样的脚趾涂成了淡淡的粉红，像小小的粉红贝壳。她的气味也是粉红的，像婴儿。她长着大女孩的手，骨头却像女人的骨头一样细长。她也化了妆。可她不会系鞋带。我会。

有时很晚了，我仍听到他们在笑，听到啤酒罐响和猫叫，还有树儿在窃窃私语：等呀等呀等吧。塞尔让罗伊丝绕着街区骑他的自行车，有时他们一起散步。我望着他们。她牵他的手，他有时停下来帮她系鞋带。妈妈说这样的女孩，这样的女孩是会钻进小巷里去胡来的女孩。不会系鞋带的罗伊丝。他把她带去了哪里？

我身体里的每样东西都屏住了呼吸。每样东西都在等待像圣诞节一样绽放。我想做一个焕然一新的我。我想要晚上坏坏地坐在外面,脖子上挽个男孩,裙子下有风吹过。不是像这样,每晚都对着树说话,欠身窗外,想象我看不到的事情。

有一次一个男孩紧紧抱着我,我发誓,我感到他手臂的握力与重量,可那是在梦里。

塞尔。你是怎么抱她的?抱着,像这样?你什么时候吻了她?像这样?

四棵细瘦的树

它们是唯一懂得我的。我是唯一懂得它们的。四棵细瘦的树长着细细的脖颈和尖尖的肘骨,像我的一样。不属于这里但到了这里的四个。市政栽下充数的四棵残次品。从我的房间里我们可以听到它们的声音,可蕾妮只是睡觉,不能领略这些。

它们的力量是个秘密。它们在地下展开凶猛的根系。它们向上生长也向下生长,用它们须发样的脚趾攥紧泥土,用它们猛烈的牙齿噬咬天空,怒气从不懈怠。这就是它们坚持的方式。

假如有一棵忘记了它存在的理由,它们就全都会像玻璃瓶里的郁金香一样耷拉下来,手挽着手。坚持,坚持,坚持。树儿在我睡着的时候说。它们教会人。

当我太悲伤太瘦弱无法坚持再坚持的时候,当我如此渺小却要对抗这么多砖块的时候,我就会看着树。当街上没有别的东西可看的时候。不畏水泥仍在生长的四棵。伸展伸展从不忘记伸展的四棵。唯一的理由是存在存在的四棵。

别说英语

玛玛西塔是街对面三楼正面公寓里那个男人的大个儿妈妈。拉切尔说她的名字应该是玛玛索塔，我想这不重要。

那个男人攒钱把她接到了这里。他攒呀攒呀，因为她一个人带着小男娃在那个国家生活。他做两份工。他早出晚归。每一天。

后来有一天，玛玛西塔和小男娃坐一辆黄色出租车来了。出租车门像侍者的手臂一样打开。迈出来一只粉色小鞋，一只兔子耳朵一样柔嫩的脚。接着是肥肥的脚踝、扇动的臀、紫红玫瑰和绿色香水。那个男人得在外面拉,出租车司机得在里面推,推呀拉呀,推呀拉。出来了!

一瞬间她像花一样打开了。庞大,大得惊人,却看上去很美,从帽顶上的浅橙色羽毛到脚趾上的小玫瑰花苞。我简直没法把眼睛从她的小鞋上移开。

上去,上去,她抱着蓝色毯子里的小男娃走上了楼梯。男人拎着她的衣箱、紫色帽盒,十几盒缎面高跟鞋。然后,我们就看不到她了。

有人说是因为她太胖,有人说是因为那三层楼梯,可我认为她不出来是因为害怕说英语,可能是这样的,因为她只知道八个单词。房东来的时候,她知道说:他不在;如果是别的人去,她就会说,"别说英语",还有"见鬼"。我不知道她从哪里学的这个,但我听她说过一次,感到很惊讶。

我父亲说他刚到这个国家的时候吃了三个月的火腿煎蛋。早餐、午餐和晚餐都是。火腿煎蛋。他就知道这个单词。他再也不吃火腿煎蛋了。

不管是什么原因,是因为她胖呢,或是不想爬楼,还是怕说英语呢,反正她都不会下来。她整天坐在窗边收听西班牙语广播节目,唱各种关于她的国家的思乡曲,声音听起来像只海鸥。

　　家。家。家是照片里的一所房子，一所粉红色的房子，粉红得像一朵休目光线下的蜀葵。男人把寓所的墙壁都漆成了粉红色，可那是不一样的，你知道。她依然在为她粉红色的房子叹息。后来，我想，她哭了。是我我会的。

　　有时男人厌烦了。他嘶喊起来，整条街都能听到。

　　唉。她说。她很伤心。

　　哦。他说。再也不喊了。

　　唉。什么时候，什么时候，什么时候？她问。

　　唉。他娘的！我们是在家里。这就是家。我人在这里，我住在这里。说英语。说英语。上帝！

　　唉！玛玛西塔，不属于这里的人，时不时地发出一声哭喊，歇斯底里的，高声的，似乎他扯断了她最后一丝维系生命的线，一条通向那个国家唯一的出路。

　　后来，永远地伤了她的心的是，那个小男娃，开始说话了，开始唱他在电视上听到的百事可乐广告歌。

　　别讲英语。她对那个操着那种听起来像马口铁的语言在唱歌的孩子说。别讲英语，别讲英语，然后泪如泉涌。别，别，别，她好像不能相信自己的耳朵。

在星期二喝可可和木瓜汁的拉菲娜

每逢星期二，拉菲娜的丈夫回家就晚，因为这一晚他要玩多米诺骨牌。于是拉菲娜，年纪轻轻就因为倚在窗口太久太久而变老的她，被锁在了屋里，因为她的丈夫害怕拉菲娜会逃跑，因为她长得太美，不能被人看到。

拉菲娜倚在窗口，倚着她的胳膊肘，梦想她的头发能像拉潘索公主[42]的一样。酒吧的乐声从街角传来，拉菲娜希望能在变老以前去那里，去跳舞。

时间过去很久了，我们忘了她在那上面张望，直到她说：孩子们，我给你们一元钱，你们去店里帮我买点东西好吗?她扔下一张皱巴巴的票子来。她总是要可可汁,有时要木瓜汁。我们把它放进一个她用晾衣绳放下来的纸手袋里,给她递上去。

星期二总是喝可可汁或木瓜汁的拉菲娜希望生活里有更甜的饮料,不像一间空屋子那么苦涩,而是像小岛,像街那头的舞厅一样甜美。在舞厅里,比她老很多的女人可以像掷色子一样随意地抛媚眼,用钥匙开家里的门。并且总会有人过来献上更甜美的饮料,承诺把它们用银色绳子系起来[43]。

---

42 Rapunzel,拉潘索公主。《格林童话》中的长发少女,她被巫婆诅咒,囚禁在高塔里。后来她放下长发让王子爬上来与之幽会。几经曲折,她终于获得了自由和爱情。"Rapunzel"在德语里是"野莴苣"的意思,因此中译本《格林童话》里大都翻成"莴苣姑娘"。
43 用银色绳子系起来的饮料表达了一种讽喻:可怜的拉菲娜梦想着的不过是要依附于一个更好的男人,住进一座更精美的牢笼,只是晾衣绳换成了银绳子。

萨莉

萨莉是一个描着埃及的眼圈，穿烟灰色尼龙丝袜的女孩。学校的男生认为她很美，因为她的头发像渡鸦羽毛一样乌黑闪亮，她笑的时候，把头发往后一甩，像一面滑缎方巾披在肩膀上，然后大笑起来。

她爸爸说长这么美是麻烦事。他们非常严格地遵从他的信仰。他们不能去跳舞。他想起他的姐妹们，很伤心。于是她就不能出来。我说的是萨莉。

萨莉，是谁教会你把眼睛涂得像克莉奥帕特拉[44]?如果我把这个小刷子用舌头卷一下，舔成尖尖的，蘸到小泥饼里去,那个小红盒子里的,你会教我吗?

我喜欢你的黑色外套和你穿的那些鞋。你在哪里买的?我妈妈说这么年轻穿黑色太冒险了,可我就想要买你那样的鞋,像你的那双黑色小羊皮鞋,就和那些一样的。等哪天我妈妈心情好的时候,也许我的下一个生日之后,我还会要求买一双尼龙长袜。

切芮儿,她再也不是你的朋友了,从复活节前的那个星期二起,从你弄得她的耳朵流血那天起,从她那样骂你,并在你手臂上咬了个洞的那天起,你看上去好像要哭,大家都在等着,可你没有哭,萨莉,从那时起,你没有一个最好的朋友可以一起靠在学校操场的栅栏上,可以跟着你嘲笑男孩子们说的话。没有人会借给你她的梳子。

男孩们在衣帽间里讲的事情,它们不是真的。你独自倚靠在操场的栅栏上,闭起眼睛,仿佛没有人在看,仿佛没有人能看到你站在那里,萨莉。你把眼睛那样闭起来时在想什么?为什么一放学你总是得直接回家?你变成了一个不同的萨莉。你把裙子拉直。你擦去了眼皮上的蓝色眼影。你不笑,萨莉。你低头看着脚, 飞快地走进你不会从里面出来的房子。

萨莉,你有时会希望自己可以不回家吗?你希望有一天你的脚可以走呀走,把你远远地带出芒果街,远远地,也许你的脚会停下来,在一所房子前,一所美丽的房子,有鲜花和大窗,还有你可以两级并一级跳上去的台阶。台阶上面有一个等你到来的房间。如果你拔掉小窗的插销,轻轻一推,窗就打开了,所有的天空都会涌进来。那里不会有爱管闲事的邻居在张望,不会有摩托和汽车,不会有床单、毛巾和洗衣店。只有树,更多的树,还有足够的蓝天。你会笑出来,萨莉。你睡去醒来时不用去想谁喜欢你谁不喜欢你。你合上眼睛不用担心别人说了些什么,因为你毕竟从来不属于这里。没有人会使你伤心,没有人会认为你怪,只因你喜欢做梦做梦;没有人会冲你叫喊,只因他们看到你在黑暗里倚靠着一辆小汽车;倚靠着某个人而没有人觉得你坏,没有人说这是错的,没有一整个世界都在等你犯错误,而你想要的,你想要的,萨莉,只是爱爱爱爱,没有人会把这说成是疯狂。

44 古代埃及女王,以美貌著称于世,罗马统帅恺撒和安东尼曾先后迷恋于她,后埃及灭国时以毒蛇噬己自尽。深而大的眼圈是她以及当时的埃及女人最显著的妆容特点。

密涅瓦写诗

密涅瓦只比我大一点点,可她已经有两个孩子和一个出走的丈夫。她妈妈独自抚养了孩子们,看来她的女儿也要走她的老路了。因为她运气这样糟,密涅瓦哭呀哭。每个夜晚每个白天。并且祈祷。不过,在喂完孩子们煎饼晚餐后,他们就睡着了,她会在小纸片上写诗。那纸片她折了又折,捏在手里很长时间了,闻起来像一角硬币的小纸片。

她让我读她的诗。我让她读我的。她总是悲伤得像一所着了火的房子——总是有什么出了问题。她麻烦太多了,最大的麻烦就是她丈夫会出走,而且不停地出走。

一天她不想再忍了,她让他知道够了就是够了。从门里出去的是他。从窗户里出去的是他的衣服、唱片和鞋子,门锁上了。可那晚他又回来了,从窗户扔进来一块大石头。然后他很难过,她就又开了门。老故事。

过了一个星期她浑身青紫地跑过来问她该怎么办。密涅瓦。我不知道她该往哪去。我毫无办法。

阁楼上的流浪者

我想要一所山上的房子,像爸爸工作的地方那样的花园房。星期日,爸爸的休息日,我们会去那里。我过去常去。现在不去了。你长大了,就不喜欢和我们一起出去吗?爸爸说。你傲起来了。蕾妮说。我没告诉他们我很羞愧——我们一帮人全都盯着那里的窗户,像饥饿的人。我厌倦了盯着我不能拥有的东西。如果我们赢了彩票……妈妈才开口,我就不要听了。

那些住在山上、睡得靠星星如此近的人,他们忘记了我们这些住在地面上的人。他们根本不朝下看,除非为了体会住在山上的心满意足。上星期的垃圾,对老鼠的恐惧,这些与他们无关。夜晚来临,没什么惊扰他们的梦,除了风。

有一天我要拥有自己的房子,可我不会忘记我是谁我从哪里来。路过的流浪者会问,我可以进来吗?我会把他们领上阁楼,请他们住下来,因为我知道没有房子的滋味。

有些日子里,晚饭后,我和朋友们坐在火旁。楼上的地板吱呀吱呀响。阁楼上有咕咕哝哝的声音。

是老鼠吗?他们会问。

是流浪者。我会回答说。我会很开心。

美丽的和残酷的

我是一个丑丫头。我是那个没人来要的丫头。

蕾妮说她不会一辈子等一个丈夫来要她,密涅瓦的姐姐生了个宝宝,才离开了她妈妈的家,可她不想走她的路。她想要事事随她的意, 她要挑挑拣拣。蕾妮长着漂亮的眼睛。如果你很漂亮,那么说当然就很容易了。

我妈妈说等我长大点的时候,我涩涩的头发会变得清亮,我穿的上衣会一直干净整洁。可我决定不要长大变成像别人那么温顺的样子, 把脖子搁在门槛上等待甜蜜的枷链[45]。

电影里总有一个嘴唇红红、美丽又残酷的女人。是她让男人发狂,是她大笑着让男人落荒而逃。她的力量是她自己的。她不会放弃它。

我已经开始了我自己的沉默的战争。简单。坚定。我是那个像男人一样离开餐桌的人,不把椅子摆正来,也不拾起碗筷来。

---

45 Ball and chain,甜蜜的枷链。英语习语,用以指称在亲密关系中,对你构成束缚的那个人,比如,妻子、丈夫或女友等。

一个聪明人

我本来可以出人头地的,你知道么?妈妈说着叹了口气。她一辈子都住在这个城市里。她会说两种语言。她会唱歌剧。她知道怎么修理电视机。可她不知道坐哪条地铁线去市中心。在等对的那趟车来的时候,我紧紧攥着她的手。

她过去有时间就常画画。现在她用针和线画画,编织的玫瑰花苞、丝绣的郁金香。有一天她想去看芭蕾舞。又有一天她想去看戏。她从公共图书馆里借来了歌剧唱片,用醇厚的嗓音唱起来,歌声像朝阳一样蓬勃。

今天煮燕麦片时,她是蝴蝶夫人,直到她叹了口气,用木勺指着我。我本来可以出人头地的。你知道么?埃斯佩朗莎。你去上学,用功学习。蝴蝶夫人是个傻瓜。她搅了搅燕麦。看看我的姐妹们。她说的是跑了丈夫的伊佐拉和死了丈夫的约兰达。全得靠自己撑着。她边说边摇头。

然后又没头没尾地说上了:

羞耻感是不好的,你知道。它会让你心情不好。你想知道我怎么辍学的吗?因为我没有好衣服。没有衣服,可我有脑子啊。

唉。她气恼地说着,又搅起麦片来。我那时是个聪明人。

萨莉说的

他从来没有打我很重。她说她妈妈往所有痛的地方抹猪油。然后到了学校,她会说她摔跤了。这是所有那些淤青的来历。这是她的皮肤上总有疤痕的原因。

可是谁信她。一个那么大的姑娘,一个走进来时漂亮的脸上满是青紫伤痕的姑娘,那不可能是掉下楼梯摔的。他从来没有打我很重。

可萨莉没告诉大家那次他像揍一条狗一样用手揍她,她说,好像我是一个动物。他认为我会像他的妹妹们一样私奔,使家庭蒙羞。只是因为我是个女儿,接着她就不说了。

萨莉得到允许将和我们住一阵子,星期四她终于来了,带着一布袋衣服和一纸袋她妈妈拿的甜面包。本来她可以住下来的,可天黑的时候她爸爸来了,眼睛哭肿了,变得很小,他敲打着门说请回来吧。这是最后一次。她应了一声爸爸,就回家了。

然后我们就不用担心了。直到有一天,萨莉的爸爸抓到她和一个男孩说话,第二天她没来上学。第三天也没有。直到后来萨莉说起来,他简直就是疯了,解开了皮带的他,忘记了他是她的父亲。

你不是我的女儿,你不是我的女儿。然后他挥动了手。

猴子花园

猴子再也不住那里了。猴子搬走了,去了肯塔基,带着它的家人。我很开心,因为晚上再也不用听它的狂嘶乱叫,听它的主人们嘭嚓嚓摇滚乐般的动静。那绿色的金属笼子,陶瓷桌面,那说话声音跟吉他似的一家人。猴子,一家人,桌子。都消失了。

从那时起我们接管了花园。以前我们不敢走进去,因为猴子在那里尖叫,并且龇出它黄黄的牙齿。

那里有向日葵,大得像火星上的花儿;还有肥厚的鸡冠,花朵漫溢出来像剧院帷幔上深红的裙边。那里有令人头晕的蜜蜂和打着领结的果蝇翻着跟头,在空中嗡嗡鸣唱。还有很甜很甜的桃树。还有刺玫瑰、大蓟和梨树。野草多得像眯眼睛的星星,蹭得你脚踝痒痒的,直到你用肥皂和水洗净。还有大个青苹果,硬得像膝盖。到处都是那种令人昏昏欲睡的气味:腐烂的木头、潮湿的泥土,以及那蒙了灰尘的蜀葵,像老去的人那白到发蓝的金发一样浓密而馥郁。

　　翻开石头,就会有黄色的蜘蛛逃窜出去,畏光且无明的苍白蠕虫在它们的沉睡中翻卷起来。用一根小棍插进沙土里,就会出来几只蓝色的甲虫。还有一路蚂蚁,还有那么多的壳儿脆脆的瓢虫。这是一个花园,看着它,是春天里的一件赏心乐事。可是,慢慢地,从猴子走后,花园就开始自作主张了。花儿不再规矩地待在防止它们长过小径的小砖头后面,野草混了进来。废弃的小汽车像蘑菇一样一夜之间就冒了出来。先是一辆,又来了一辆,然后是那辆没了挡风玻璃的浅蓝色皮卡车[46]。不知不觉,猴子花园里充满了沉睡的汽车。

　　花园里的东西在以某种方式消失,好像是花园自己把它们给吃了,要不就是它的老头记性,把东西收起来就忘掉了。在牵牛花爬过的那面石墙下的两块石头中间,蕾妮发现了一元钱和一只死老鼠。有一次,我们捉迷藏时,埃迪·法加斯头枕在一棵木槿树下,像瑞普·凡·温克尔[47]那样睡了过去,直到有人想起来他还在躲迷藏,才回去找他。

这个,我想,就是我们去那里的原因。远得让妈妈找不到我们。我们,还有几条住在空车子里的老狗。有一次,我们在那辆蓝色旧皮卡车的后斗里设了个俱乐部。还有,我们喜欢从一辆车顶跳到另一辆车顶,假装它们是巨大的蘑菇。

渐渐起来一种传言,说别的事物都还没出现之前,这里便有了猴子花园。我们很乐意去想,这个花园可以把东西藏上一千年。在湿漉漉的花儿的根下面,躺着被谋杀的海盗和恐龙的骨头,而独角兽的眼睛变成了煤。

这里是我曾经想死去的地方,是那天我试过去死的地方,可是,连猴子花园都不愿意收留我。那将是我最后一天去那里。

是谁说我太大了不能玩这样的游戏了?是谁的话我没有听?我只记得,别人都跑开时,我也想跑,跑上跑下蹿遍猴子花园,像男孩一样快,而不是像萨莉那样,看到袜子上沾了泥巴就尖叫。

我说,萨莉,来呀。可她没动。她待在路边和提陀还有他的朋友们说话。你想和小孩们玩,那你就玩吧。她说。我留在这里。她想要傲慢的话,就能傲慢起来。于是我离开了。

那也是她自己的错。我回来时,萨莉正在假装生气……好像是男孩们偷了她的钥匙。请还给我。她说着,用一只柔软的拳头捶打着最近的那个。他们都笑开了。她也是。那是一个我不懂的玩笑。

我想回去和别的孩子一起玩,他们还在汽车上跳来跳去,还在花园里互相追逐。可萨莉有她自己的游戏。

一个男孩设计了规则。提陀的一个朋友说,除非你亲我们,要不就拿不回钥匙。萨莉一开始假装很生气,然后就说好吧。就那么简单。

我不知道为什么。我身体里有什么东西想要扔树枝。有什么东西想要说不,当我看到萨莉走进花园里去,而提陀的伙伴们都在坏笑时。只是亲一下。就好了。每人亲一下。这有什么呢?她说。

可是,我不知道为什么心里很愤怒。好像有什么不对劲。萨莉走到那辆蓝色旧车后面去亲男孩,拿回她的钥匙,而我却跑上三层楼梯到了提陀家住的地方。他妈妈在熨衬衫。她用一个空的汽水瓶往上喷水,同时抽着一支烟。

你儿子和他的朋友偷了萨莉的钥匙,不还给她,除非她亲他们。现在他们就在让她亲他们,爬完三层楼后的我累得上气不接下气地说。

那些个小家伙。她说,头都没抬一下,继续熨着。

就这样吗?

你想要我做什么呢,她说,叫警察?然后继续熨衣服。

我瞪着她很久,可想不出要说什么,于是跑下三层楼梯回花园,到需要解救的萨莉那里去。我拿了三根大树枝和一块砖头,心想这些应该够了。

可我到了那里,萨莉说回家吧。那些男孩说走开。我手里拿着砖头觉得自己很蠢。他们都那么瞧着我,好像我才是那个做蠢事的人。这让我觉得很羞愧。

然后我不知道为什么我得跑开。我得把自己藏在花园的另一边,藏在树丛里,一棵不会介意我躺下来哭很久的树下面。我使劲把眼睛闭起来,像最渺小的星星那样,好让自己不哭。可我还是哭了。我的脸在发烫。身体里的每样东西都在呃逆。

我在哪里读到过的,在印度,有的祭司可以凭借意志让自己的心脏停跳。我也想用意志让自己的血停止流,心停止跳。我想要死去,化成雨,想要我的眼睛融化,像两条黑蜗牛一样溶进土里。我想呀想呀,闭上眼睛一心一意地想。等我站起来时,我的裙子变绿了,头也痛了起来。

我看着自己穿着白袜和圆鞋的脚。它们好像很遥远,似乎不再是我的脚了。花园曾经是那么好玩的去处,可现在似乎也不是我的了。

46 一种结合了小型货车和轿车特点的实用车型,车前部形似轿车,后面有车斗。
47 Rip Van Winkle,典出华盛顿·欧文(1783—1859)《见闻札记》中的名篇"瑞普·凡·温克尔"。山村农夫温克尔善良懦弱、好酒惧内,一日在山中遇一捐酒老翁,被酒香诱至深谷,见一众奇服异秉的怪人默然会神于九柱戏。老翁加入其中后,温克尔捺不住酒瘾,偷尝仙酒,酣然入睡,岂知这一睡便睡过了独立战争,醒来已是二十年后,家中物是人非,悍妇故去,世上沧桑巨变,新政初行。温克尔找到嫁为人妇的女儿,从此在村中住下来,向过往的旅人讲述自己的奇遇。《见闻札记》被认为是美国本土文学的开山之作,欧文也因此被称为"美国文学之父"。此书国内早有译本。

红色小丑

萨莉,你撒谎。根本不是你说的那样。他所做的。他碰我哪里。我不想要那样,萨莉。他们是那么说的,我是那么以为的,所有的故事书和电影,你们为什么对我撒谎?

我在红色小丑旁边等着。我站在你说的摩天转轮旁边。可不管怎样我不喜欢嘉年华会。我和你一起去,因为你在转轮上笑,你头向后仰哈哈大笑。我拿着你的零钱,挥着手,数你过去多少次。那些男孩都看着你,因为你漂亮。我喜欢和你在一起,萨莉。你是我的朋友。可那个大男孩,他把你带到哪儿去了?我等了那么长时间。我听了你的话,等在红色小丑旁,可你一直没来,你一直没来找我。

萨莉萨莉都一百遍了。为什么我喊你你听不到?为什么你不叫他们让我一个人待着?那个抓着我胳膊的人,他不让我走。他说我爱你,西班牙姑娘,我爱你,然后把他酸酸的嘴唇按在我的嘴唇上面。

萨莉,让他停下。我没法让他们走开。我除了哭什么都做不了。我不记得了。天黑了。我不记得了。我不记得了。请别让我说出全部。

为什么你丢下我一个人在那里?我好像等了一辈子。你是个撒谎者。他们都在撒谎。所有的书和杂志,所有的那么乱讲的人和物。只有他脏乎乎的指头压在我的皮肤上,他那酸酸的气味又来了。俯望的月亮。摩天转轮。红色的小丑发出粗哑的笑声。

然后颜色开始旋转,天空倾斜了。他们穿着高高的黑色体操鞋跑开了。萨莉,你撒谎,你撒谎。他不放我走。他说我爱你,我爱你,西班牙姑娘。

亚麻地毡上的玫瑰

萨莉结婚了,像我们知道她会的那样,年纪轻轻还没点准备可照样结婚了。她在一个学校义卖场上遇到一个药蜀葵推销员,就和他到另外一个州结了婚,因为那里在八年级前结婚是合法的。她现在有了丈夫和房子,有了枕套和餐具。她说她在恋爱,可我想她这么做是为了逃避。

萨莉说她喜欢结了婚的生活,因为现在丈夫给她钱,她可以给自己买东西。她很快乐,除了有时她丈夫会发脾气,有次还用脚踢穿了门,可大多数日子他还过得去;除了他不让她在电话上聊天。他不让她朝窗外看。他不喜欢她的朋友们,所以除了他上班去的时候,没人去看她。

　　她坐在家里,因为她不敢没有他的允许就出门。她看着他们拥有的全部:他们的毛巾、烤面包机、闹钟和窗帘。她喜欢看着墙壁,看墙角的接缝多么整齐,看亚麻地毡上的玫瑰,看平滑如婚礼蛋糕的天花板。

三姐妹

她们和八月里吹来的风一起来到,像蛛网那么轻渺,不易为人知晓。除了月亮,似乎和其他任何事物都不相关的三个。[48]一个笑声像铁皮,一个有着猫一样的眼,一个的手像瓷。婶婶们。三姐妹。妈妈们[49]。他们说。

婴儿死了。露西和拉切尔的小妹妹。有天晚上一条狗哭了,第二天一只黄色的鸟飞进了打开的窗户。那个星期还没过完,宝宝烧得更厉害了。然后耶稣来了,把宝宝带到远方去了。她们的妈妈这么说。

然后客人来了……在小屋里穿进穿出。很难让地板保持干净。过去想知道墙壁是什么颜色的人来了一批又一批,看着那个糖果盒一样的盒子里拇指般的小人。

我以前从来没看到过死人,没看过真的,像这样躺在某个人的客厅里,等着人们来亲吻和祝福,并点上一支蜡烛的。这样在一所房子里的。这好像有点奇怪。

她们一定是知道了,那三姐妹。她们有那种能力,能够感觉出什么是什么。她们说,过来,给了我一条香口胶。她们身上的气味像面纸,又像一个丝缎手袋里面的味道。于是我不觉得害怕。

你叫什么名字,那个长着猫眼的问。

埃斯佩朗莎。我说。

埃斯佩朗莎。那个老而且青筋突起的用一种尖细的声音重复着。埃斯佩朗莎……多好的名字。

我的膝盖疼。那个笑声滑稽的抱怨说。

明天要下雨了。

是的,明天。她们说。

你们怎么知道?我问。

我们知道。

看看她的手。猫眼说。

于是她们把我的手翻过来翻过去,好像在找什么东西一样。

她很特别。

是的,她会去很远的地方。

是的,是的,嗯。

许个愿吧。

许愿?

是的,许个愿。你想要什么?

什么都可以?我问。

是的,为什么不是?

我闭上了眼睛。

你许好了吗?

是的。我说。

好,就这样,它会实现的。

你怎么知道?我问。

我们知道。我们知道。

埃斯佩朗莎。那个长着大理石样的手的把我叫到一旁。埃斯佩朗莎。她用她青筋突起的手捧着我的脸,看了又看。许久的沉默。你离开时总要记得回来。她说。

什么?

你离开时要记得为了其他人回来。一个圈子。懂吗?你永远是埃斯佩朗莎。你永远是芒果街的人。你不能忘记你知道的事情。你不能忘记你是谁。

然后我不知道说什么好。她似乎能看懂我的心思。她似乎知道我刚才许下了什么愿。我为许下那么自私的一个愿望感到羞愧。

你要记得回来。为了那些不像你那么容易离开的人。你会记得吗?她那么问我似乎是在告诉我。是的,是的。我有点迷糊地说。

好。她说,揉了揉我的手。好。就这样。你可以走了。

我站起来走到露西和拉切尔一起去,她们已经等在门外了,正在奇怪我和那三个散发着肉桂气味的老女人做什么。她们告诉我的事情我不是都明白。我转过身。她们微笑着,挥了挥手,用她们轻烟似的姿态。

后来我就没见过她们了。一次也没有,两次也没有。从此再也没有。

48　在墨西哥的土著文明里,月神就是女人的神。这里将三姐妹与月亮联系起来,增加了一层神秘寓意。
49　原文为西班牙文,*las comadres*,对应的英文是 co-mothers。这个词更加突出了这三姐妹形象中的神话原型意味。

阿莉西娅和我
在埃德娜的台阶上交谈

我喜欢阿莉西娅,因为她有次给了我一个小皮包,上面绣着瓜达拉哈拉[50]的字样。那里是阿莉西娅的家,有一天她会回到那里。可今天她在倾听我的忧伤,因为我没有一所房子。

你就住在这里呀,芒果街4006。阿莉西娅说着指向那栋让我羞愧的小屋。

不,那不是我的房子,我说着,摇了摇头,像是这一摇便可以抹去我在那里住过的一年。我不属于。我从来不想来自那里。你有一个家,阿莉西娅,有一天你会去那里,去一个你记得的城市，可我从来没有一所房子，连一张照片都没有……只有梦到的那所。

不。阿莉西娅说。不管你喜欢与否,你都是芒果街的,有一天你也要回来的。

我不会。除非有人让它变好了。

谁来做这事？市长吗？

市长来芒果街的想法让我大笑起来。

谁来做这事？不是市长。

---

50 墨西哥第二大城市,哈利科斯州首府,2005年度"美洲文化之都",始建于1531年,以其优雅民风、深厚文化传统和龙舌兰酒闻名于世,被认为是墨西哥最高贵的城市。

一所我自己的房子

不是小公寓。也不是阴面的大公寓。也不是哪一个男人的房子。也不是爸爸的。是完完全全我自己的。那里有我的前廊我的枕头,我漂亮的紫色矮牵牛。我的书和我的故事。我的两只等在床边的鞋。不用和谁去作对。没有别人扔下的垃圾要拾起。

只是一所寂静如雪的房子,一个自己归去的空间,洁净如同诗笔未落的纸。

芒果有时说再见

我喜欢讲故事。我在心里讲述。在邮递员说过这是你的邮件之后。这是你的邮件。他说。然后我开始讲述。

我编了一个故事,为我的生活,为我棕色鞋子走过的每一步。我说:"她步履沉重地登上木楼梯,她悲哀的棕色鞋子带着她走进了她从来不喜欢的房子。"

我喜欢讲故事。我将向你们讲述一个不想归属的女孩的故事。

我们先前不住芒果街。先前我们住鲁米斯的三楼。再先前我们住吉勒。吉勒前面是波琳娜。可我记得最清楚的是芒果街,悲哀的红色小屋。我住在那里却不属于那里的房子。

我把它写在纸上,然后心里的幽灵就不那么疼了。我把它写下来,芒果有时说再见。她不再用双臂抱住我。她放开了我。

有一天我会把一袋袋的书和纸打进包里。有一天我会对芒果说再见。我强大得她没法永远留住我。有一天我会离开。

朋友和邻居们会说,埃斯佩朗莎怎么了?她带着这么多书和纸去哪里?为什么她要走得那么远?

他们不会知道,我离开是为了回来。为了那些我留在身后的人。为了那些无法出去的人。

The House on Mango Street

A las Mujeres

To the Women

The House on Mango Street

We didn't always live on Mango Street. Before that we lived on Loomis on the third floor, and before that we lived on Keeler. Before Keeler it was Paulina, and before that I can't remember. But what I remember most is moving a lot. Each time it seemed there'd be one more of us. By the time we got to Mango Street we were six—Mama, Papa, Carlos, Kiki, my sister Nenny and me.

The house on Mango Street is ours, and we don't have to pay rent to anybody, or share the yard with the people downstairs, or be careful not to make too much noise, and there isn't a landlord banging on the ceiling with a broom. But even so, it's not the house we'd thought we'd get.

We had to leave the flat on Loomis quick. The water pipes broke and the landlord wouldn't fix them because the house was too old. We had to leave fast. We were using the washroom next door and carrying water over in empty milk gallons. That's why Mama and Papa looked for a house, and that's why we moved into the house on Mango Street, far away, on the other side of town.

They always told us that one day we would move into a house, a real house that would be ours for always so we wouldn't have to move each year. And our house would have running water and pipes that worked. And inside it would have real stairs, not hallway stairs, but stairs inside like the houses on T.V. And we'd have a basement and at least three washrooms so when we took a bath we wouldn't have to tell everybody. Our house would be white with trees around it, a great big yard and grass growing without a fence. This was the house Papa talked about when he held a lottery ticket and this was the house Mama dreamed up in the stories she told us before we went to bed.

But the house on Mango Street is not the way they told it at all. It's small and red with tight steps in front and windows so small you'd think they were holding their breath. Bricks are crumbling in places, and the front door is so swollen you have to push hard to get in. There is no front yard, only four little elms the city planted by the curb. Out back is a small garage for the car we don't own yet and a small yard that looks smaller between the two buildings on either side. There are stairs in our house, but they're ordinary hallway stairs, and the house has only one washroom. Everybody has to share a bedroom—Mama and Papa, Carlos and Kiki, me and Nenny.

Once when we were living on Loomis, a nun from my school passed by and saw me playing out front. The laundromat downstairs had been boarded up because it had been robbed two days before and the owner had painted on the wood YES WE'RE OPEN so as not to lose business.

Where do you live? She asked.

There, I said pointing up to the third floor.

You live *there*?

There. I had to look to where she pointed—the third floor, the paint peeling, wooden bars Papa had nailed on the windows so we wouldn't fall out. You live *there*? The way she said it made me feel like nothing. *There.* I lived *there.* I nodded.

I knew then I had to have a house. A real house. One I could point to. But this isn't it. The house on Mango Street isn't it. For the time being, Mama says. Temporary, says Papa. But I know how those things go.

Hairs

Everybody in our family has different hair. My Papa's hair is like a broom, all up in the air. And me, my hair is lazy. It never obeys barrettes or bands. Carlos' hair is thick and straight. He doesn't need to comb it. Nenny's hair is slippery—slides out of your hand. And Kiki, who is the youngest, has hair like fur.

But my mother's hair, my mother's hair, like little rosettes, like little candy circles all curly and pretty because she pinned it in pincurls all day, sweet to put your nose into when she is holding you, holding you and you feel safe, is the warm smell of bread before you bake it, is the smell when she makes room for you on her side of the bed still warm with her skin, and you sleep near her, the rain outside falling and Papa snoring. The snoring, the rain, and Mama's hair that smells like bread.

Boys & Girls

The boys and the girls live in separate worlds. The boys in their universe and we in ours. My brothers for example. They've got plenty to say to me and Nenny inside the house. But outside they can't be seen talking to girls. Carlos and Kiki are each other's best friend... not ours.

Nenny is too young to be my friend. She's just my sister and that was not my fault. You don't pick your sisters, you just get them and sometimes they come like Nenny.

She can't play with those Vargas kids or she'll turn out just like them. And since she comes right after me, she is my responsibility.

Someday I will have a best friend all my own. One I can tell my secrets to. One who will understand my jokes without my having to explain them. Until then I am a red balloon, a balloon tied to an anchor.

My Name

In English my name means hope. In Spanish it means too many letters. It means sadness, it means waiting. It is like the number nine. A muddy color. It is the Mexican records my father plays on Sunday mornings when he is shaving, songs like sobbing.

It was my great-grandmother's name and now it is mine. She was a horse woman too, born like me in the Chinese year of the horse—which is supposed to be bad luck if you're born female—but I think this is a Chinese lie because the Chinese, like the Mexicans, don't like their women strong.

My great-grandmother. I would've liked to have known her, a wild horse of a woman, so wild she wouldn't marry. Until my great-grandfather threw a sack over her head and carried her off. Just like that, as if she were a fancy chandelier. That's the way he did it.

And the story goes she never forgave him. She looked out the window her whole life, the way so many women sit their sadness on an elbow. I wonder if she made the best with what she got or was she sorry because she couldn't be all the things she wanted to be. Esperanza. I have inherited her name, but I don't want to inherit her place by the window.

At school they say my name funny as if the syllables were made out of tin and hurt the roof of your mouth. But in Spanish my name is made out of a softer something, like silver, not quite as thick as sister's name—Magdalena—which is uglier than mine. Magdalena who at least can come home and become Nenny. But I am always Esperanza.

I would like to baptize myself under a new name, a name more like the real me, the one nobody sees. Esperanza as Lisandra or Maritza or Zeze the X. Yes. Something like Zeze the X will do.

Cathy
Queen of Cats

She says, I am the great great grand cousin of the queen of France. She lives upstairs, over there, next door to Joe the baby-grabber. Keep away from him, she says. He is full of danger. Benny and Blanca own the corner store. They're okay except don't lean on the candy counter. Two girls raggedy as rats live across the street. You don't want to know them. Edna is the lady who owns the building next to you. She used to own a building big as a whale, but her brother sold it. Their mother said no, no, don't ever sell it. I won't. And then she closed her eyes and he sold it. Alicia is stuck-up ever since she went to college. She used to like me but now she doesn't.

Cathy who is queen of cats has cats and cats and cats. Baby cats, big cats, skinny cats, sick cats. Cats asleep like little donuts. Cats on top of the refrigerator. Cats taking a walk on the dinner table. Her house is like cat heaven.

You want a friend, she says. Okay, I'll be your friend. But only till next Tuesday. That's when we move away. Got to. Then as if she forgot I just moved in, she says the neighborhood is getting bad.

Cathy's father will have to fly to France one day and find her great great distant grand cousin on her father's side and inherit the family house. How do I know this is so? She told me so. In the meantime they'll just have to move a little farther north from Mango Street, a little farther away every time people like us keep moving in.

Our Good Day

If you give me five dollars I will be your friend forever. That's what the little one tells me.

Five dollars is cheap since I don't have any friends except Cathy who is only my friend till Tuesday.

Five dollars, five dollars.

She is trying to get somebody to chip in so they can buy a bicycle from this kid named Tito. They already have ten dollars and all they need is five more.

Only five dollars, she says.

Don't talk to them, says Cathy. Can't you see they smell

like a broom.

But I like them. Their clothes are crooked and old. They are wearing shiny Sunday shoes without socks. It makes their bald ankles all red, but I like them. Especially the big one who laughs with all her teeth. I like her even though she lets the little one do all the talking.

Five dollars, the little one says, only five.

Cathy is tugging my arm and I know whatever I do next will make her mad forever.

Wait a minute, I say, and run inside to get the five dollars. I have three dollars saved and I take two of Nenny's. She's not home, but I'm sure she'll be glad when she finds out we own a bike. When I get back, Cathy is gone like I knew she would be, but I don't care. I have two new friends and a bike too.

My name is Lucy, the big one says. This here is Rachel my sister.

I'm her sister, says Rachel. Who are you?

And I wish my name was Cassandra or Alexis or Maritza—anything but Esperanza—but when I tell them my name they don't laugh.

We come from Texas, Lucy says and grins. Her was born here, but me I'm Texas.

You mean *she*, I say.

No, I'm from Texas, and doesn't get it.

This bike is three ways ours, says Rachel who is thinking ahead already. Mine today, Lucy's tomorrow and yours day after.

But everybody wants to ride it today because the bike is new, so we decide to take turns *after* tomorrow. Today it belongs to all of us.

I don't tell them about Nenny just yet. It's too complicated. Especially since Rachel almost put out Lucy's eye about who was going to get to ride it first. But finally we agree to ride it together. Why not?

Because Lucy has long legs she pedals. I sit on the back seat and Rachel is skinny enough to get up on the handlebars which makes the bike all wobbly as if the wheels are spaghetti, but after a bit you get used to it.

We ride fast and faster. Past my house, sad and red and crumbly in places, past Mr. Benny's grocery on the corner, and down the avenue which is dangerous. Laundromat, junk store, drugstore, windows and cars and more cars, and around the block back to Mango.

People on the bus wave. A very fat lady crossing the street says, You sure got quite a load there.

Rachel shouts, You got quite a load there too. She is very sassy.

Down, down Mango Street we go. Rachel, Lucy, me. Our new bicycle. Laughing the crooked ride back.

Laughter

Nenny and I don't look like sisters... not right away. Not the way you can tell with Rachel and Lucy who have the same fat popsicle lips like everybody else in their family. But me and Nenny, we are more alike than you would know. Our laughter for example. Not the shy ice cream bells' giggle of Rachel and Lucy's family, but all of a sudden and surprised like a pile of dishes breaking. And other things I can't explain.

One day we were passing a house that looked, in my mind, like houses I had seen in Mexico. I don't know why. There was nothing about the house that looked exactly like the houses I remembered. I'm not even sure why I thought it, but it seemed to feel right.

Look at that house, I said, it looks like Mexico.

Rachel and Lucy look at me like I'm crazy, but before they can let out a laugh, Nenny says: Yes, that's Mexico all right. That's what I was thinking exactly.

Gil's
Furniture
Bought & Sold

There is a junk store. An old man owns it. We bought a used refrigerator from him once, and Carlos sold a box of magazines for a dollar. The store is small with just a dirty window for light. He doesn't turn the lights on unless you got money to buy things with, so in the dark we look and see all kinds of things, me and Nenny. Tables with their feet upside-down and rows and rows of refrigerators with round corners and couches that spin dust in the air when you punch them and a hundred T.V.'s that don't work probably. Everything is on top of everything so the whole store has skinny aisles to walk through. You can get lost easy.

The owner, he is a black man who doesn't talk much and sometimes if you didn't know better you could be in there a long time before your eyes notice a pair of gold glasses floating in the dark. Nenny who thinks she is smart and talks to any old man, asks lots of questions. Me, I never said nothing to him except once when I bought the Statue of Liberty for a dime.

But Nenny, I hear her asking one time how's this here and the man says, This, this is a music box, and I turn around quick thinking he means a *pretty* box with flowers painted on it, with a ballerina inside. Only there's nothing like that where this old man is pointing, just a wood box that's old and got a big brass record in it with holes. Then he starts it up and all sorts of things start happening. It's like all of a sudden he let go a million moths all over the dusty furniture and swan-neck shadows and in our bones. It's like drops of water. Or like marimbas only with a funny little plucked sound to it like if you were running your fingers across the teeth of a metal comb.

And then I don't know why, but I have to turn around and pretend I don't care about the box so Nenny won't see how stupid I am. But Nenny, who is stupider, already is asking how much and I can see her fingers going for the quarters in her pants pocket.

This, the old man says shutting the lid, this ain't for sale.

Meme Ortiz

Meme Ortiz moved into Cathy's house after her family moved away. His name isn't really Meme. His name is Juan. But when we asked him what his name was he said Meme, and that's what everybody calls him except his mother.

Meme has a dog with gray eyes, a sheepdog with two names, one in English and one in Spanish. The dog is big, like a man dressed in a dog suit, and runs the same way its owner does, clumsy and wild and with the limbs flopping all over the place like untied shoes.

Cathy's father built the house Meme moved into. It is

wooden. Inside the floors slant. Some rooms uphill. Some down. And there are no closets. Out front there are twenty-one steps, all lopsided and jutting like crooked teeth (made that way on purpose, Cathy said, so the rain will slide off), and when Meme's mama calls from the doorway, Meme goes scrambling up the twenty-one wooden stairs with the dog with two names scrambling after him.

Around the back is a yard, mostly dirt, and a greasy bunch of boards that used to be a garage. But what you remember most is this tree, huge, with fat arms and mighty families of squirrels in the higher branches. All around, the neighborhood of roofs, black-tarred and A-framed, and in their gutters, the balls that never came back down to earth. Down at the base of the tree, the dog with two names barks into the empty air, and there at the end of the block, looking smaller still, our house with its feet tucked under like a cat.

This is the tree we chose for the First Annual Tarzan Jumping Contest. Meme won. And broke both arms.

Louie,
His Cousin
&
His Other Cousin

Downstairs from Meme's is a basement apartment that Meme's mother fixed up and rented to a Puerto Rican family. Louie's family. Louie is the oldest in a family of little sisters. He is my brother's friend really, but I know he has two cousins and that his T-shirts never stay tucked in his pants.

Louie's girl cousin is older than us. She lives with Louie's family because her own family is in Puerto Rico. Her name is Marin or Maris or something like that, and she wears dark nylons all the time and lots of makeup she gets free from selling Avon. She can't come out—gotta baby-sit with Louie's sisters—but she stands in the doorway a lot, all the time singing, clicking her fingers, the same song:

> *Apples, peaches, pumpkin pah-ay.*
> *You're in love and so am ah-ay.*

Louie has another cousin. We only saw him once, but it was important. We were playing volleyball in the alley when he drove up in this great big yellow Cadillac with whitewalls and a yellow scarf tied around the mirror. Louie's cousin had his arm out the window. He honked a couple of times and a lot of faces looked out from Louie's back window and then a lot of people came out—Louie, Marin and all the little sisters.

Everybody looked inside the car and asked where he got it. There were white rugs and white leather seats. We all asked for a ride and asked where he got it. Louie's cousin said get in.

We each had to sit with one of Louie's little sisters on our lap, but that was okay. The seats were big and soft like a sofa, and there was a little white cat in the back window whose eyes lit up when the car stopped or turned. The windows didn't roll up like in ordinary cars. Instead there was a button that did it for you automatically. We rode up the alley and around the block six times, but Louie's cousin said he was going to make us walk home if we didn't stop playing with the windows or touching the FM radio.

The seventh time we drove into the alley we heard sirens... real quiet at first, but then louder. Louie's cousin stopped the car right where we were and said, Everybody out of the car. Then he took off flooring that car into a yellow blur. We hardly had time to think when the cop car pulled in the alley going just as fast. We saw the yellow Cadillac at the end of the block trying to make a left-hand turn, but our alley is too skinny and the car crashed into a lamppost.

Marin screamed and we ran down the block to where the cop car's siren spun a dizzy blue. The nose of that yellow Cadillac was all pleated like an alligator's, and except for a bloody lip and a bruised forehead, Louie's cousin was okay. They put handcuffs on him and put him in the backseat of the cop car, and we all waved as they drove away.

Marin

Marin's boyfriend is in Puerto Rico. She shows us his letters and makes us promise not to tell anybody they're getting married when she goes back to P.R. She says he didn't get a job yet, but she's saving the money she gets from selling Avon and taking care of her cousins.

Marin says that if she stays here next year, she's going to get a real job downtown because that's where the best jobs are, since you always get to look beautiful and get to wear nice clothes and can meet someone in the subway who might marry you and take you to live in a big house far away.

But next year Louie's parents are going to send her back to her mother with a letter saying she's too much trouble, and that is too bad because I like Marin. She is older and knows lots of things. She is the one who told us how Davey the Baby's sister got pregnant and what cream is best for taking off moustache hair and if you count the white flecks on your fingernails you can know how many boys are thinking of you and lots of other things I can't remember now.

We never see Marin until her aunt comes home from work, and even then she can only stay out in front. She is there every night with the radio. When the light in her aunt's room goes out, Marin lights a cigarette and it doesn't matter if it's cold out or if the radio doesn't work or if we've got nothing to say to each other. What matters, Marin says, is for the boys to see us and for us to see them. And since Marin's skirts are shorter and since her eyes are pretty, and since Marin is already older than us in many ways, the boys who do pass by say stupid things like I am in love with those two green apples you call eyes, give them to me why don't you. And Marin just looks at them without even blinking and is not afraid.

Marin, under the streetlight, dancing by herself, is singing the same song somewhere. I know. Is waiting for a car to stop, a star to fall, someone to change her life.

Those
Who Don't

Those who don't know any better come into our neighborhood scared. They think we're dangerous. They think we will attack them with shiny knives. They are stupid people who are lost and got here by mistake.

But we aren't afraid. We know the guy with the crooked eye is Davey the Baby's brother, and the tall one next to him in the straw brim, that's Rosa's Eddie V., and the big one that looks like a dumb grown man, he's Fat Boy, though he's not fat anymore nor a boy.

All brown all around, we are safe. But watch us drive into

a neighborhood of another color and our knees go shakity-shake and our car windows get rolled up tight and our eyes look straight. Yeah. That is how it goes and goes.

There Was an Old Woman She Had So Many Children She Didn't Know What to Do

Rosa Vargas' kids are too many and too much. It's not her fault you know, except she is their mother and only one against so many.

They are bad those Vargases, and how can they help it with only one mother who is tired all the time from buttoning and bottling and babying, and who cries every day for the man who left without even leaving a dollar for bologna or a note explaining how come.

The kids bend trees and bounce between cars and dangle upside down from knees and almost break like fancy museum vases you can't replace. They think it's funny. They are without respect for all things living, including themselves.

But after a while you get tired of being worried about kids who aren't even yours. One day they are playing chicken on Mr. Benny's roof. Mr. Benny says, Hey ain't you kids know better than to be swinging up there? Come down, you come down right now, and then they just spit.

See. That's what I mean. No wonder everybody gave up. Just stopped looking out when little Efren chipped his buck tooth on a parking meter and didn't even stop Refugia from getting her head stuck between two slats in the back gate and nobody looked up not once the day Angel Vargas learned to fly and dropped from the sky like a sugar donut, just like a falling star, and exploded down to earth without even an "Oh."

Alicia
Who Sees Mice

Close your eyes and they'll go away, her father says, or You're just imagining. And anyway, a woman's place is sleeping so she can wake up early with the tortilla star, the one that appears early just in time to rise and catch the hind legs hide behind the sink, beneath the four-clawed tub, under the swollen floorboards nobody fixes, in the corner of your eyes.

Alicia, whose mama died, is sorry there is no one older to rise and make the lunchbox tortillas. Alicia, who inherited her mama's rolling pin and sleepiness, is young and smart and studies for the first time at the university. Two trains and a bus, because she doesn't want to spend her whole life in a factory or behind a rolling pin. Is a good girl, my friend, studies all night and sees the mice, the ones her father says do not exist. Is afraid of nothing except four-legged fur. And fathers.

Darius
&
the Clouds

You can never have too much sky. You can fall asleep and wake up drunk on sky, and sky can keep you safe when you are sad. Here there is too much sadness and not enough sky. Butterflies too are few and so are flowers and most things that are beautiful. Still, we take what we can get and make the best of it.

Darius, who doesn't like school, who is sometimes stupid and mostly a fool, said something wise today, though most days he says nothing. Darius, who chases girls with firecrackers or a stick that touched a rat and thinks he's tough, today pointed up because the world was full of clouds, the kind like pillows.

    You all see that cloud, that fat one there? Darius said, See that? Where? That one next to the one that look like popcorn. That one there. See that. That's God, Darius said. God? somebody little asked. God, he said, and made it simple.

And Some More

    The Eskimos got thirty different names for snow, I say. I read it in a book.

    I got a cousin, Rachel says. She got three different names.

    There ain't thirty different kinds of snow, Lucy says. There are two kinds. The clean kind and the dirty kind, clean and dirty. Only two.

    There are a million zillion kinds, says Nenny. No two exactly alike. Only how do you remember which one is which?

    She got three last names and, let me see, two first names.

One in English and one in Spanish...

And clouds got at least ten different names, I say.

Names for clouds? Nenny asks. Names just like you and me?

That up there, that's cumulus, and everybody looks up.

Cumulus are cute, Rachel says. She *would* say something like that.

What's that one there? Nenny asks, pointing a finger.

That's cumulus too. They're all cumulus today. Cumulus, cumulus, cumulus.

No, she says. That there is Nancy, otherwise known as Pig-eye. And over there her cousin Mildred, and little Joey, Marco, Nereida and Sue.

There are all different kinds of clouds. How many different kinds of clouds can you think of?

Well, there's these already that look like shaving cream...

And what about the kind that looks like you combed its hair? Yes, those are clouds too.

Phyllis, Ted, Alfredo and Julie...

There are clouds that look like big fields of sheep, Rachel

says. Them are my favorite.

And don't forget nimbus the rain cloud, I add, that's something.

Jose and Dagoberto, Alicia, Raul, Edna, Alma and Rickey...

There's that wide puffy cloud that looks like your face when you wake up after falling asleep with all your clothes on.

Reynaldo, Angelo, Albert, Armando, Mario...

Not my face. Looks like your fat face.

Rita, Margie, Ernie...

Whose fat face?

Esperanza's fat face, that's who. Looks like Esperanza's ugly face when she comes to school in the morning.

Anita, Stella, Dennis, and Lolo...

Who you calling ugly, ugly?

Richie, Yolanda, Hector, Stevie, Vincent...

Not you. Your mama, that's who.

My mama? You better not be saying that, Lucy Guerrero. You better not be talking like that... else you can say goodbye to being my friend forever.

I'm saying your mama's ugly like... ummm...

... like bare feet in September!

That does it! Both of yous better get out of my yard before I call my brothers.

Oh, we're only playing.

I can think of thirty Eskimo words for you, Rachel. Thirty words that say what you are.

Oh yeah, well I can think of some more.

Uh-oh, Nenny. Better get the broom. Too much trash in our yard today.

Frankie, Licha, Maria, Pee Wee...

Nenny, you better tell your sister she is really crazy because Lucy and me are never coming back here again. Forever.

Reggie, Elizabeth, Lisa, Louie...

You can do what you want to do, Nenny, but you better not talk to Lucy or Rachel if you want to be my sister.

You know what you are, Esperanza? You are like the Cream of Wheat cereal. You're like the lumps.

Yeah, and you're foot fleas, that's you.

Chicken lips.

Rosemary, Dalia, Lily...

Cockroach jelly.

Jean, Geranium and Joe...

Cold *frijoles*.

Mimi, Michael, Moe...

Your mama's *frijoles*.

Your ugly mama's toes.

That's stupid.

Bebe, Blanca, Benny...

Who's stupid?

Rachel, Lucy, Esperanza, and Nenny.

The Family of Little Feet

There was a family. All were little. Their arms were little, and their hands were little, and their height was not tall, and their feet very small.

The grandpa slept on the living room couch and snored through his teeth. His feet were fat and doughy like thick tamales, and these he powdered and stuffed into white socks and brown leather shoes.

The grandma's feet were lovely as pink pearls and dressed in velvety high heels that made her walk with a wobble, but she wore them anyway because they were pretty.

The baby's feet had ten tiny toes, pale and see-through like a salamander's, and these he popped into his mouth whenever he was hungry.

The mother's feet, plump and polite, descended like white pigeons from the sea of pillow, across the linoleum roses, down down the wooden stairs, over the chalk hopscotch squares, 5, 6, 7, blue sky.

Do you want this? And gave us a paper bag with one pair of lemon shoes and one red and one pair of dancing shoes that used to be white but were now pale blue. Here, and we said thank you and waited until she went upstairs.

Hurray! Today we are Cinderella because our feet fit exactly, and we laugh at Rachel's one foot with a girl's grey sock and a lady's high heel. Do you like these shoes? But the truth is it is scary to look down at your foot that is no longer yours and see attached a long long leg.

Everybody wants to trade. The lemon shoes for the red shoes, the red for the pair that were once white but are now pale blue, the pale blue for the lemon, and take them off and put them back on and keep on like this a long time until we are tired.

Then Lucy screams to take our socks off and yes, it's true. We have legs. Skinny and spotted with satin scars where scabs were picked, but legs, all our own, good to look at, and long.

It's Rachel who learns to walk the best all strutted in those magic high heels. She teaches us to cross and uncross our legs, and to run like a double-dutch rope, and how to walk down to the corner so that the shoes talk back to you with every step. Lucy, Rachel, me tee-tottering like so. Down to the corner where the men can't take their eyes off us. We must be Christmas.

Mr. Benny at the corner grocery puts down his important cigar: Your mother know you got shoes like that? Who give you those?

Nobody.

Them are dangerous, he says. You girls too young to be wearing shoes like that. Take them shoes off before I call the cops, but we just run.

On the avenue a boy on a homemade bicycle calls out: Ladies, lead me to heaven.

But there is nobody around but us.

Do you like these shoes? Rachel says yes, and Lucy says yes, and yes I say, these are the best shoes. We will never go back to wearing the other kind again. Do you like these shoes?

In front of the laundromat six girls with the same fat face pretend we are invisible. They are the cousins, Lucy says, and always jealous. We just keep strutting.

Across the street in front of the tavern a bum man on the stoop.

Do you like these shoes?

Bum man says, Yes, little girl. Your little lemon shoes are so beautiful. But come closer. I can't see very well. Come closer. Please.

You are a pretty girl, bum man continues. What's your name, pretty girl?

And Rachel says Rachel, just like that.

Now you know to talk to drunks is crazy and to tell them your name is worse, but who can blame her. She is young and dizzy to hear so many sweet things in one day, even if it is a bum man's whiskey words saying them.

Rachel, you are prettier than a yellow taxicab. You know that?

But we don't like it. We got to go, Lucy says.

If I give you a dollar will you kiss me? How about a dollar. I give you a dollar, and he looks in his pocket for wrinkled money.

We have to go right now, Lucy says taking Rachel's hand because she looks like she's thinking about that dollar.

Bum man is yelling something to the air but by now we are running fast and far away, our high heel shoes taking us all the way down the avenue and around the block, past the ugly cousins, past Mr. Benny's, up Mango Street, the back way, just in case.

We are tired of being beautiful. Lucy hides the lemon shoes and the red shoes and the shoes that used to be white but are now pale blue under a powerful bushel basket on the back porch, until one Tuesday her mother, who is very clean, throws them away. But no one complains.

A
Rice Sandwich

The special kids, the ones who wear keys around their necks, get to eat in the canteen. The canteen! Even the name sounds important. And these kids at lunch time go there because their mothers aren't home or home is too far away to get to.

My home isn't far but it's not close either, and somehow I got it in my head one day to ask my mother to make me a sandwich and write a note to the principal so I could eat in the canteen too.

Oh no, she says pointing the butter knife at me as if I'm

starting trouble, no sir. Next thing you know everybody will be wanting a bag lunch—I'll be up all night cutting bread into little triangles, this one with mayonnaise, this one with mustard, no pickles on mine, but mustard on one side please. You kids just like to invent more work for me.

But Nenny says she doesn't want to eat at school—ever—because she likes to go home with her best friend Gloria who lives across the schoolyard. Gloria's mama has a big color T.V. and all they do is watch cartoons. Kiki and Carlos, on the other hand, are patrol boys. They don't want to eat at school either. They like to stand out in the cold especially if it's raining. They think suffering is good for you ever since they saw that movie *300 Spartans*.

I'm no Spartan and hold up an anemic wrist to prove it. I can't even blow up a balloon without getting dizzy. And besides, I know how to make my own lunch. If I ate at school there'd be less dishes to wash. You would see me less and less and like me better. Everyday at noon my chair would be empty. Where is my favorite daughter you would cry, and when I came home finally at three p.m. you would appreciate me.

Okay, okay, my mother says after three days of this. And the following morning I get to go to school with my mother's letter and a rice sandwich because we don't have lunch meat.

Mondays or Fridays, it doesn't matter, mornings always go by slow and this day especially. But lunchtime came finally and I got to get in line with the stay-at-school kids. Everything is fine until the nun who knows all the canteen kids by heart looks at me and says: You, who sent you here? And since I am shy, I don't say anything, just hold out my hand with the letter. This is no good, she says, till Sister Superior gives the okay. Go upstairs and see her. And so I went.

I had to wait for two kids in front of me to get hollered at, one because he did something in class, the other because he didn't. My turn came and I stood in front of the big desk with holy pictures under the glass while the Sister Superior read my letter. It went like this:

Dear Sister Superior,

Please let Esperanza eat in the lunchroom because she lives too far away and she gets tired. As you can see she is very skinny. I hope to God she does not faint.

> Thanking you,
> Mrs. E. Cordero

You don't live far, she says. You live across the boulevard. That's only four blocks. Not even. Three maybe. Three long blocks away from here. I bet I can see your house from my window. Which one? Come here. Which one is your house?

And then she made me stand up on a box of books and point. That one? she said, pointing to a row of ugly three-flats, the ones even the raggedy men are ashamed to go into. Yes, I nodded even though I knew that wasn't my house and started to cry. I always cry when nuns yell at me, even if they're not yelling.

Then she was sorry and said I could stay—just for today, not tomorrow or the day after—you go home. And I said yes and could I please have a Kleenex—I had to blow my nose.

In the canteen, which was nothing special, lots of boys and girls watched while I cried and ate my sandwich, the bread already greasy and the rice cold.

Chanclas

It's me—Mama, Mama said. I open up and she's there with bags and big boxes, the new clothes and, yes, she's got the socks and a new slip with a little rose on it and a pink-and-white striped dress. What about the shoes? I forgot. Too late now. I'm tired. Whew!

Six-thirty already and my little cousin's baptism is over. All day waiting, the door locked, don't open up for nobody, and I don't till Mama gets back and buys everything except the shoes.

Now Uncle Nacho is coming in his car, and we have to

hurry to get to Precious Blood Church quick because that's where the baptism party is, in the basement rented for today for dancing and tamales and everyone's kids running all over the place.

Mama dances, laughs, dances. All of a sudden, Mama is sick. I fan her hot face with a paper plate. Too many tamales, but Uncle Nacho says too many this and tilts his thumb to his lips.

Everybody laughing except me, because I'm wearing the new dress, pink and white with stripes, and new underclothes and new socks and the old saddle shoes I wear to school, brown and white, the kind I get every September because they last long and they do. My feet scuffed and round, and the heels all crooked that look dumb with this dress, so I just sit.

Meanwhile that boy who is my cousin by first communion or something asks me to dance and I can't. Just stuff my feet under the metal folding chair stamped Precious Blood and pick on a wad of brown gum that's stuck beneath the seat. I shake my head no. My feet growing bigger and bigger.

Then Uncle Nacho is pulling and pulling my arm and it

doesn't matter how new the dress Mama bought is because my feet are ugly until my uncle who is a liar says, You are the prettiest girl here, will you dance, but I believe him, and yes, we are dancing, my Uncle Nacho and me, only I don't want to at first. My feet swell big and heavy like plungers, but I drag them across the linoleum floor straight center where Uncle wants to show off the new dance we learned. And Uncle spins me, and my skinny arms bend the way he taught me, and my mother watches, and my little cousins watch, and the boy who is my cousin by first communion watches, and everyone says, wow, who are those two who dance like in the movies, until I forget that I am wearing only ordinary shoes, brown and white, the kind my mother buys each year for school.

And all I hear is the clapping when the music stops. My uncle and me bow and he walks me back in my thick shoes to my mother who is proud to be my mother. All night the boy who is a man watches me dance. He watched me dance.

Hips

I like coffee, I like tea.
I like the boys and the boys like me.
Yes, no, maybe so. Yes, no, maybe so...

One day you wake up and they are there. Ready and waiting like a new Buick with the keys in the ignition. Ready to take you where?

They're good for holding a baby when you're cooking, Rachel says, turning the jump rope a little quicker. She has no imagination.

You need them to dance, says Lucy.

If you don't get them you may turn into a man. Nenny says this and she believes it. She is this way because of her age.

That's right, I add before Lucy or Rachel can make fun of her. She is stupid alright, but she *is* my sister.

But most important, hips are scientific, I say repeating what Alicia already told me. It's the bones that let you know which skeleton was a man's when it was a man and which a woman's.

They bloom like roses, I continue because it's obvious I'm the only one who can speak with any authority; I have science on my side. The bones just one day open. Just like that. One day you might decide to have kids, and then where are you going to put them? Got to have room. Bones got to give.

But don't have too many or your behind will spread. That's how it is, says Rachel whose mama is as wide as a boat. And we just laugh.

What I'm saying is who here is ready? You gotta be able to know what to do with hips when you get them, I say making it up as I go. You gotta know how to walk with hips, practice you know—like if half of you wanted to go one way and the other half the other.

That's to lullaby it, Nenny says, that's to rock the baby asleep inside you. And then she begins singing *seashells, copper bells eevy, ivy, o-ver.*

I'm about to tell her that's the dumbest thing I've ever heard, but the more I think about it...

You gotta get the rhythm, and Lucy begins to dance. She has the idea, though she's having trouble keeping her end of the double-dutch steady.

It's gotta be just so, I say. Not too fast and not too slow. Not too fast and not too slow.

We slow the double circles down to a certain speed so Rachel who has just jumped in can practice shaking it.

I want to shake like hoochi-coochie, Lucy says. She is crazy.

I want to move like heebie-jeebie, I say picking up on the cue.

I want to be Tahiti. Or *merengue*. Or electricity.

Or *tembleque!*

Yes, *tembleque*. That's a good one.
And then it's Rachel who starts it:

> *Skip, skip,*
> *snake in your hips.*
> *Wiggle around*
> *and break your lip.*

Lucy waits a minute before her turn. She is thinking. Then she begins:

> *The waitress with the big fat hips*
> *who pays the rent with taxi tips...*
> *says nobody in town will kiss her on the lips*
> *because...*
> *because she looks like Christopher Columbus!*
> *Yes, no, maybe so. Yes, no, maybe so.*

She misses on maybe so. I take a little while before my turn, take a breath, and dive in:

> *Some are skinny like chicken lips.*
> *Some are baggy like soggy Band-Aids*
> *after you get out of the bathtub.*
> *I don't care what kind I get.*
> *Just as long as I get hips.*

Everybody getting into it now except Nenny who is still humming *not a girl, not a boy, just a little baby*. She's like that.

When the two arcs open wide like jaws Nenny jumps in across from me, the rope tick-ticking, the little gold earrings our mama gave her for her First Holy Communion bouncing. She is the color of a bar of naphtha laundry soap, she is like the little brown piece left at the end of the wash, the hard little bone, my sister. Her mouth opens. She begins:

> *My mother and your mother were washing clothes.*
> *My mother punched your mother right in the nose.*
> *What color blood came out?*

Not that old song, I say. You gotta use your own song. Make it up, you know? But she doesn't get it or won't. It's hard to say which. The rope turning, turning, turning.

> *Engine, engine number nine,*
> *running down Chicago line.*
> *If the train runs off the track*
> *do you want your money back?*
> *Do you want your MONEY back?*
> *Yes, no, maybe so. Yes, no, maybe so...*

I can tell Lucy and Rachel are disgusted, but they don't say anything because she's *my* sister.

> *Yes, no, maybe so. Yes, no, maybe so...*

Nenny, I say, but she doesn't hear me. She is too many light-years away. She is in a world we don't belong to anymore. Nenny. Going. Going.

> *Y-E-S spells yes and out you go!*

The
First Job

It wasn't as if I didn't want to work. I did. I had even gone to the social security office the month before to get my social security number. I needed money. The Catholic high school cost a lot, and Papa said nobody went to public school unless you wanted to turn out bad.

I thought I'd find an easy job, the kind other kids had, working in the dime store or maybe a hotdog stand. And though I hadn't started looking yet, I thought I might the week after next. But when I came home that afternoon, all wet because Tito had pushed me into the open water hydrant—only I had sort of let him—Mama called me in the kitchen before I could even go and change, and Aunt Lala was sitting there drinking her coffee with a spoon. Aunt Lala said she had found a job for me at the Peter Pan Photo Finishers on North Broadway where she worked, and how old was I, and to show up tomorrow saying I was one year older, and that was that.

So the next morning I put on the navy blue dress that made me look older and borrowed money for lunch and bus fare because Aunt Lala said I wouldn't get paid till the next Friday, and I went in and saw the boss of the Peter Pan Photo Finishers on North Broadway where Aunt Lala worked and lied about my age like she told me to and sure enough, I started that same day.

In my job I had to wear white gloves. I was supposed to match negatives with their prints, just look at the picture and look for the same one on the negative strip, put it in the envelope, and do the next one. That's all. I didn't know where these envelopes were coming from or where they were going. I just did what I was told.

It was real easy, and I guess I wouldn't have minded it except that you got tired after a while and I didn't know if I could sit down or not, and then I started sitting down only when the two ladies next to me did. After a while they started to laugh and came up to me and said I could sit when I wanted to, and I said I knew.

When lunchtime came, I was scared to eat alone in the company lunchroom with all those men and ladies looking, so I ate real fast standing in one of the washroom stalls and had lots of time left over, so I went back to work early. But then break time came, and not knowing where else to go, I went into the coatroom because there was a bench there.

I guess it was the time for the night shift or middle shift to arrive because a few people came in and punched the time clock, and an older Oriental man said hello and we talked for a while about my just starting, and he said we could be friends and next time to go in the lunchroom and sit with him, and I felt better. He had nice eyes and I didn't feel so nervous anymore. Then he asked if I knew what day it was, and when I said I didn't, he said it was his birthday and would I please give him a birthday kiss. I thought I would because he was so old and just as I was about to put my lips on his cheek, he grabs my face with both hands and kisses me hard on the mouth and doesn't let go.

Papa
Who Wakes Up Tired
in the Dark

Your *abuelito* is dead, Papa says early one morning in my room. *Está muerto*, and then as if he just heard the news himself, crumples like a coat and cries, my brave Papa cries. I have never seen my Papa cry and don't know what to do.

I know he will have to go away, that he will take a plane to Mexico, all the uncles and aunts will be there, and they will have a black-and-white photo taken in front of the tomb with flowers shaped like spears in a white vase because this is how they send the dead away in that country.

Because I am the oldest, my father has told me first, and

now it is my turn to tell the others. I will have to explain why we can't play. I will have to tell them to be quiet today.

My Papa, his thick hands and thick shoes, who wakes up tired in the dark, who combs his hair with water, drinks his coffee, and is gone before we wake, today is sitting on my bed.

And I think if my own Papa died what would I do. I hold my Papa in my arms. I hold and hold and hold him.

Born Bad

Most likely I will go to hell and most likely I deserve to be there. My mother says I was born on an evil day and prays for me. Lucy and Rachel pray too. For ourselves and for each other... because of what we did to Aunt Lupe.

Her name was Guadalupe and she was pretty like my mother. Dark. Good to look at. In her Joan Crawford dress and swimmer's legs. Aunt Lupe of the photographs.

But I knew her sick from the disease that would not go, her legs bunched under the yellow sheets, the bones gone limp as worms. The yellow pillow, the yellow smell, the bottles and spoons. Her head thrown back like a thirsty lady. My aunt, the swimmer.

Hard to imagine her legs once strong, the bones hard and parting water, clean sharp strokes, not bent and wrinkled like a baby, not drowning under the sticky yellow light. Second-floor rear apartment. The naked light bulb. The high ceilings. The light bulb always burning.

I don't know who decides who deserves to go bad. There was no evil in her birth. No wicked curse. One day I believe she was swimming, and the next day she was sick. It might have been the day that gray photograph was taken. It might have been the day she was holding cousin Totchy and baby Frank. It might have been the moment she pointed to the camera for the kids to look and they wouldn't.

Maybe the sky didn't look the day she fell down. Maybe God was busy. It could be true she didn't dive right one day and hurt her spine. Or maybe the story that she fell very hard from a high step stool, like Totchy said, is true.

But I think diseases have no eyes. They pick with a dizzy finger anyone, just anyone. Like my aunt who happened to be walking down the street one day in her Joan Crawford dress, in her funny felt hat with the black feather, cousin Totchy in one hand, baby Frank in the other.

Sometimes you get used to the sick and sometimes the sickness, if it is there too long, gets to seem normal. This is how it was with her, and maybe this is why we chose her.

It was a game, that's all. It was the game we played every afternoon ever since that day one of us invented it—I can't remember who—I think it was me.

You had to pick somebody. You had to think of someone everybody knew. Someone you could imitate and everyone else would have to guess who it was. It started out with famous people: Wonder Woman, the Beatles, Marilyn Monroe. ... But then somebody thought it'd be better if we changed the game a little, if we pretended we were Mr. Benny, or his wife Blanca, or Ruthie, or anybody we knew.

I don't know why we picked her. Maybe we were bored that day. Maybe we got tired. We liked my aunt. She listened to our stories. She always asked us to come back. Lucy, me, Rachel. I hated to go there alone. The six blocks to the dark apartment, second-floor rear building where sunlight never came, and what did it matter? My aunt was blind by then. She never saw the dirty dishes in the sink. She couldn't see the ceilings dusty with flies, the ugly maroon walls, the bottles and sticky spoons. I can't forget the smell. Like sticky capsules filled with jelly. My aunt, a little oyster, a little piece of meat on an open shell for us to look at. Hello, hello. As if she had fallen into a well.

I took my library books to her house. I read her stories. I liked the book *The Waterbabies*. She liked it too. I never knew how sick she was until that day I tried to show her one of the pictures in the book, a beautiful color picture of the water babies swimming in the sea. I held the book up to her face. I can't see it, she said, I'm blind. And then I was ashamed.

She listened to every book, every poem I read her. One day I read her one of my own. I came very close. I whispered it into the pillow:

> *I want to be*
> *like the waves on the sea,*

> *like the clouds in the wind,*
> *but I'm me.*
> *One day I'll jump*
> *out of my skin.*
> *I'll shake the sky*
> *like a hundred violins.*

That's nice. That's very good, she said in her tired voice. You just remember to keep writing, Esperanza. You must keep writing. It will keep you free, and I said yes, but at that time I didn't know what she meant.

The day we played the game, we didn't know she was going to die. We pretended with our heads thrown back, our arms limp and useless, dangling like the dead. We laughed the way she did. We talked the way she talked, the way blind people talk without moving their head. We imitated the way you had to lift her head a little so she could drink water, she sucked it up slow out of a green tin cup. The water was warm and tasted like metal. Lucy laughed. Rachel too. We took turns being her. We screamed in the weak voice of a parrot for

Totchy to come and wash those dishes. It was easy.

We didn't know. She had been dying such a long time, we forgot. Maybe she was ashamed. Maybe she was embarrassed it took so many years. The kids who wanted to be kids instead of washing dishes and ironing their papa's shirts, and the husband who wanted a wife again.

And then she died, my aunt who listened to my poems.

And then we began to dream the dreams.

Elenita, Cards, Palm, Water

Elenita, witch woman, wipes the table with a rag because Ernie who is feeding the baby spilled Kool-Aid. She says: Take that crazy baby out of here and drink your Kool-Aid in the living room. Can't you see I'm busy? Ernie takes the baby into the living room where Bugs Bunny is on T.V.

Good lucky you didn't come yesterday, she says. The planets were all mixed up yesterday.

Her T.V. is color and big and all her pretty furniture made out of red fur like the teddy bears they give away in carnivals. She has them covered with plastic. I think this is on account of the baby.

Yes, it's a good thing, I say.

But we stay in the kitchen because this is where she works. The top of the refrigerator busy with holy candles, some lit, some not, red and green and blue, a plaster saint and a dusty Palm Sunday cross, and a picture of the voodoo hand taped to the wall.

Get the water, she says.

I go to the sink and pick the only clean glass there, a beer mug that says the beer that made Milwaukee famous, and fill it up with hot water from the tap, then put the glass of water on the center of the table, the way she taught me.

Look in it, do you see anything?

But all I see are bubbles.

You see anybody's face?

Nope, just bubbles, I say.

That's okay, and she makes the sign of the cross over the water three times and then begins to cut the cards.

They're not like ordinary playing cards, these cards. They're strange, with blond men on horses and crazy baseball bats with thorns. Golden goblets, sad-looking women dressed in old-fashioned dresses, and roses that cry.

There is a good Bugs Bunny cartoon on T.V. I know, I saw it before and recognize the music and wish I could go sit on the plastic couch with Ernie and the baby, but now my fortune begins. My whole life on that kitchen table: past, present, future. Then she takes my hand and looks into my palm. Closes it. Closes her eyes too.

Do you feel it, feel the cold?

Yes, I lie, but only a little.

Good, she says, *los espíritus* are here. And begins.

This card, the one with the dark man on a dark horse, this means jealousy, and this one, sorrow. Here a pillar of bees and this a mattress of luxury. You will go to a wedding soon and did you lose an anchor of arms, yes, an anchor of arms? It's clear that's what that means.

What about a house, I say, because that's what I came for.

Ah, yes, a home in the heart. I see a home in the heart.

Is that *it*?

That's what I see, she says, then gets up because the kids

are fighting. Elenita gets up to hit and then hug them. She really does love them, only sometimes they are rude.

She comes back and can tell I'm disappointed. She's a witch woman and knows many things. If you got a headache, rub a cold egg across your face. Need to forget an old romance? Take a chicken's foot, tie it with red string, spin it over your head three times, then burn it. Bad spirits keeping you awake? Sleep next to a holy candle for seven days, then on the eighth day, spit. And lots of other stuff. Only now she can tell I'm sad.

Baby, I'll look again if you want me to. And she looks again into the cards, palm, water, and says uh-huh.

A home in the heart, I was right.

Only I don't get it.

A new house, a house made of heart. I'll light a candle for you.

All this for five dollars I give her.

Thank you and goodbye and be careful of the evil eye. Come back again on a Thursday when the stars are stronger. And may the Virgin bless you. And shuts the door.

Geraldo
No Last Name

She met him at a dance. Pretty too, and young. Said he worked in a restaurant, but she can't remember which one. Geraldo. That's all. Green pants and Saturday shirt. Geraldo. That's what he told her.

And how was she to know she'd be the last one to see him alive. An accident, don't you know. Hit-and-run. Marin, she goes to all those dances. Uptown. Logan. Embassy. Palmer. Aragon. Fontana. The Manor. She likes to dance. She knows how to do cumbias and salsas and rancheras even. And he was just someone she danced with. Somebody she met that night.

That's right.

That's the story. That's what she said again and again. Once to the hospital people and twice to the police. No address. No name. Nothing in his pockets. Ain't it a shame.

Only Marin can't explain why it mattered, the hours and hours, for somebody she didn't even know. The hospital emergency room. Nobody but an intern working all alone. And maybe if the surgeon would've come, maybe if he hadn't lost so much blood, if the surgeon had only come, they would know who to notify and where.

But what difference does it make? He wasn't anything to her. He wasn't her boyfriend or anything like that. Just another *brazer* who didn't speak English. Just another wetback. You know the kind. The ones who always look ashamed. And what was she doing out at three a.m. anyway? Marin who was sent home with her coat and some aspirin. How does she explain?

She met him at a dance. Geraldo in his shiny shirt and green pants. Geraldo going to a dance.

What does it matter?

They never saw the kitchenettes. They never knew about

the two-room flats and sleeping rooms he rented, the weekly money orders sent home, the currency exchange. How could they?

His name was Geraldo. And his home is in another country. The ones he left behind are far away, will wonder, shrug, remember. Geraldo—he went north... we never heard from him again.

Edna's Ruthie

Ruthie, tall skinny lady with red lipstick and blue babushka, one blue sock and one green because she forgot, is the only grown-up we know who likes to play. She takes her dog Bobo for a walk and laughs all by herself, that Ruthie. She doesn't need anybody to laugh with, she just laughs.

She is Edna's daughter, the lady who owns the big building next door, three apartments front and back. Every week Edna is screaming at somebody, and every week somebody has to move away. Once she threw out a pregnant lady just because she owned a duck... and it was a nice duck too. But

Ruthie lives here and Edna can't throw her out because Ruthie is her daughter.

Ruthie came one day, it seemed, out of nowhere. Angel Vargas was trying to teach us how to whistle. Then we heard someone whistling—beautiful like the Emperor's nightingale—and when we turned around there was Ruthie.

Sometimes we go shopping and take her with us, but she never comes inside the stores and if she does she keeps looking around her like a wild animal in a house for the first time.

She likes candy. When we go to Mr. Benny's grocery she gives us money to buy her some. She says make sure it's the soft kind because her teeth hurt. Then she promises to see the dentist next week, but when next week comes, she doesn't go.

Ruthie sees lovely things everywhere. I might be telling her a joke and she'll stop and say: The moon is beautiful like a balloon. Or somebody might be singing and she'll point to a few clouds: Look, Marlon Brando. Or a sphinx winking. Or my left shoe.

Once some friends of Edna's came to visit and asked Ruthie if she wanted to go with them to play bingo. The car motor was running, and Ruthie stood on the steps wondering whether to go. Should I go, Ma? She asked the gray shadow behind the second-floor screen. I don't care, says the screen, go if you want. Ruthie looked at the ground. What do you think, Ma? Do what you want, how should I know? Ruthie looked at the ground some more. The car with the motor running waited fifteen minutes and then they left. When we brought out the deck of cards that night, we let Ruthie deal.

There were many things Ruthie could have been if she wanted to. Not only is she a good whistler, but she can sing and dance too. She had lots of job offers when she was young, but she never took them. She got married instead and moved away to a pretty house outside the city. Only thing I can't understand is why Ruthie is living on Mango Street if she doesn't have to, why is she sleeping on a couch in her mother's living room when she has a real house all her own, but she says she's just visiting and next weekend her husband's going to take her home. But the weekends come and go and Ruthie stays. No matter. We are glad because she is our friend.

I like showing Ruthie the books I take out of the library.

Books are wonderful, Ruthie says, and then she runs her hand over them as if she could read them in braille. They're wonderful, wonderful, but I can't read anymore. I get headaches. I need to go to the eye doctor next week. I used to write children's books once, did I tell you?

One day I memorized all of "The Walrus and the Carpenter" because I wanted Ruthie to hear me. "The sun was shining on the sea, shining with all his might..." Ruthie looked at the sky and her eyes got watery at times. Finally I came to the last lines: "But answer came there none—and this was scarcely odd, because they'd eaten every one..." She took a long time looking at me before she opened her mouth, and then she said, You have the most beautiful teeth I have ever seen, and went inside.

The Earl of Tennessee

Earl lives next door in Edna's basement, behind the flower boxes Edna paints green each year, behind the dusty geraniums. We used to sit on the flower boxes until the day Tito saw a cockroach with a spot of green paint on its head. Now we sit on the steps that swing around the basement apartment where Earl lives.

Earl works nights. His blinds are always closed during the day. Sometimes he comes out and tells us to keep quiet. The little wooden door that has wedged shut the dark for so long opens with a sigh and lets out a breath of mold and dampness, like books that have been left out in the rain. This is the only time we see Earl except for when he comes and goes to work. He has two little black dogs that go everywhere with him. They don't walk like ordinary dogs, but leap and somersault like an apostrophe and comma.

At night Nenny and I can hear when Earl comes home from work. First the click and whine of the car door opening, then the scrape of concrete, the excited tinkling of dog tags, followed by the heavy jingling of keys, and finally the moan of the wooden door as it opens and lets loose its sigh of dampness.

Earl is a jukebox repairman. He learned his trade in the South, he says. He speaks with a Southern accent, smokes fat cigars and wears a felt hat—winter or summer, hot or cold, don't matter—a felt hat. In his apartment are boxes and boxes of 45 records, moldy and damp like the smell that comes out of his apartment whenever he opens the door. He gives the records away to us—all except the country and western.

The word is that Earl is married and has a wife somewhere. Edna says she saw her once when Earl brought her to the apartment. Mama says she is a skinny thing, blond and pale like salamanders that have never seen the sun. But I saw her once too and she's not that way at all. And the boys across the street say she is a tall red-headed lady who wears tight pink pants and green glasses. We never agree on what she looks like, but we do know this. Whenever she arrives, he holds her tight by the crook of the arm. They walk fast into the apartment, lock the door behind them and never stay long.

Sire

I don't remember when I first noticed him looking at me—Sire. But I knew he was looking. Every time. All the time I walked past his house. Him and his friends sitting on their bikes in front of the house, pitching pennies. They didn't scare me. They did, but I wouldn't let them know. I don't cross the street like other girls. Straight ahead, straight eyes. I walked past. I knew he was looking. I had to prove to me I wasn't scared of nobody's eyes, not even his. I had to look back hard, just once, like he was glass. And I did. I did once. But I looked too long when he rode his bike past me. I looked because I wanted to be brave, straight into the dusty cat fur of his eyes and the bike stopped and he bumped into a parked car, bumped, and I walked fast. It made your blood freeze to have somebody look at you like that. Somebody looked at me. Somebody looked. But his kind, his ways. He is a punk, Papa says, and Mama says not to talk to him.

And then his girlfriend came. Lois I heard him call her. She is tiny and pretty and smells like baby's skin. I see her sometimes running to the store for him. And once when she was standing next to me at Mr. Benny's grocery she was barefoot, and I saw her barefoot baby toenails all painted pale pale pink, like little pink seashells, and she smells pink like babies do. She's got big girl hands, and her bones are long like ladies' bones, and she wears makeup too. But she doesn't know how to tie her shoes. I do.

Sometimes I hear them laughing late, beer cans and cats and the trees talking to themselves: wait, wait, wait. Sire lets Lois ride his bike around the block, or they take walks together. I watch them. She holds his hand, and he stops sometimes to tie her shoes. But Mama says those kinds of girls, those girls are the ones that go into alleys. Lois who can't tie her shoes. Where does he take her?

Everything is holding its breath inside me. Everything is waiting to explode like Christmas. I want to be all new and shiny. I want to sit out bad at night, a boy around my neck and the wind under my skirt. Not this way, every evening talking to the trees, leaning out my window, imagining what I can't see.

A boy held me once so hard, I swear, I felt the grip and weight of his arms, but it was a dream.

Sire. How did you hold her? Was it? Like this? And when you kissed her? Like this?

Four
Skinny Trees

They are the only ones who understand me. I am the only one who understands them. Four skinny trees with skinny necks and pointy elbows like mine. Four who do not belong here but are here. Four raggedy excuses planted by the city. From our room we can hear them, but Nenny just sleeps and doesn't appreciate these things.

Their strength is secret. They send ferocious roots beneath the ground. They grow up and they grow down and grab the earth between their hairy toes and bite the sky with violent teeth and never quit their anger. This is how they keep.

Let one forget his reason for being, they'd all droop like tulips in a glass, each with their arms around the other. Keep, keep, keep, trees say when I sleep. They teach.

When I am too sad and too skinny to keep keeping, when I am a tiny thing against so many bricks, then it is I look at trees. When there is nothing left to look at on this street. Four who grew despite concrete. Four who reach and do not forget to reach. Four whose only reason is to be and be.

No
Speak English

Mamacita is the big mama of the man across the street, third-floor front. Rachel says her name ought to be *Mamasota*, but I think that's mean.

The man saved his money to bring her here. He saved and saved because she was alone with the baby boy in that country. He worked two jobs. He came home late and he left early. Every day.

Then one day *Mamacita* and the baby boy arrived in a yellow taxi. The taxi door opened like a waiter's arm. Out stepped a tiny pink shoe, a foot soft as a rabbit's ear, then the thick ankle, a flutter of hips, fuchsia roses and green perfume. The man had to pull her, the taxicab driver had to push. Push, pull. Push, pull.Poof!

All at once she bloomed. Huge, enormous, beautiful to look at, from the salmon-pink feather on the tip of her hat down to the little rosebuds of her toes. I couldn't take my eyes off her tiny shoes.

Up, up, up the stairs she went with the baby boy in a blue blanket, the man carrying her suitcases, her lavender hatboxes, a dozen boxes of satin high heels. Then we didn't see her.

Somebody said because she's too fat, somebody because of the three flights of stairs, but I believe she doesn't come out because she is afraid to speak English, and maybe this is so since she only knows eight words. She knows to say: *He not here* for when the landlord comes, *No speak English* if anybody else comes, and *Holy smokes*. I don't know where she learned this, but I heard her say it one time and it surprised me.

My father says when he came to this country he ate hamandeggs for three months. Breakfast, lunch and dinner. Hamandeggs. That was the only word he knew. He doesn't eat hamandeggs anymore.

Whatever her reasons, whether she is fat, or can't climb the stairs, or is afraid of English, she won't come down. She sits all day by the window and plays the Spanish radio show and sings all the homesick songs about her country in a voice that sounds like a seagull.

Home. Home. Home is a house in a photograph, a pink house, pink as hollyhocks with lots of startled light. The man paints the walls of the apartment pink, but it's not the same, you know. She still sighs for her pink house, and then I think she cries. I would.

Sometimes the man gets disgusted. He starts screaming and you can hear it all the way down the street.

Ay, she says, she is sad.

Oh, he says. Not again.

¿*Cuándo, cuándo, cuándo*? she asks.

¡*Ay, caray*! We *are* home. This *is* home. Here I am and here I stay. Speak English. Speak English. Christ!

¡*Ay*! *Mamacita*, who does not belong, every once in a while lets out a cry, hysterical, high, as if he had torn the only skinny thread that kept her alive, the only road out to that country.

And then to break her heart forever, the baby boy, who has begun to talk, starts to sing the Pepsi commercial he heard on T.V.

No speak English, she says to the child who is singing in the language that sounds like tin. No speak English, no speak English, and bubbles into tears. No, no, no, as if she can't believe her ears.

Rafaela Who Drinks Coconut & Papaya Juice on Tuesdays

On Tuesdays Rafaela's husband comes home late because that's the night he plays dominoes. And then Rafaela, who is still young but getting old from leaning out the window so much, gets locked indoors because her husband is afraid Rafaela will run away since she is too beautiful to look at.

Rafaela leans out the window and leans on her elbow and dreams her hair is like Rapunzel's. On the corner there is music from the bar, and Rafaela wishes she could go there and dance before she gets old.

A long time passes and we forget she is up there watching

until she says: Kids, if I give you a dollar will you go to the store and buy me something? She throws a crumpled dollar down and always asks for coconut or sometimes papaya juice, and we send it up to her in a paper shopping bag she lets down with clothesline.

Rafaela who drinks and drinks coconut and papaya juice on Tuesdays and wishes there were sweeter drinks, not bitter like an empty room, but sweet sweet like the island, like the dance hall down the street where women much older than her throw green eyes easily like dice and open homes with keys. And always there is someone offering sweeter drinks, someone promising to keep them on a silver string.

Sally

Sally is the girl with eyes like Egypt and nylons the color of smoke. The boys at school think she's beautiful because her hair is shiny black like raven feathers and when she laughs, she flicks her hair back like a satin shawl over her shoulders and laughs.

Her father says to be this beautiful is trouble. They are very strict in his religion. They are not supposed to dance. He remembers his sisters and is sad. Then she can't go out. Sally I mean.

Sally, who taught you to paint your eyes like Cleopatra?

And if I roll the little brush with my tongue and chew it to a point and dip it in the muddy cake, the one in the little red box, will you teach me?

I like your black coat and those shoes you wear, where did you get them? My mother says to wear black so young is dangerous, but I want to buy shoes just like yours, like your black ones made out of suede, just like those. And one day, when my mother's in a good mood, maybe after my next birthday, I'm going to ask to buy the nylons too.

Cheryl, who is not your friend anymore, not since last Tuesday before Easter, not since the day you made her ear bleed, not since she called you that name and bit a hole in your arm and you looked as if you were going to cry and everyone was waiting and you didn't, you didn't, Sally, not since then, you don't have a best friend to lean against the schoolyard fence with, to laugh behind your hands at what the boys say. There is no one to lend you her hairbrush.

The stories the boys tell in the coatroom, they're not true. You lean against the schoolyard fence alone with your eyes closed as if no one was watching, as if no one could see you standing there, Sally. What do you think about when you close your eyes like that? And why do you always have to go straight home after school? You become a different Sally. You pull your skirt straight, you rub the blue paint off your eyelids. You don't laugh, Sally. You look at your feet and walk fast to the house you can't come out from.

Sally, do you sometimes wish you didn't have to go home? Do you wish your feet would one day keep walking and take you far away from Mango Street, far away and maybe your feet would stop in front of a house, a nice one with flowers and big windows and steps for you to climb up two by two upstairs to where a room is waiting for you. And if you opened the little window latch and gave it a shove, the windows would swing open, all the sky would come in. There'd be no nosy neighbors watching, no motorcycles and cars, no sheets and towels and laundry. Only trees and more trees and plenty of blue sky. And you could laugh, Sally. You could go to sleep and wake up and never have to think who likes and doesn't like you. You could close your eyes and you wouldn't have to worry what people said because you never belonged here anyway and nobody could make you sad and nobody would think you're strange because you like to dream and dream. And no one could yell at you if they saw you out in the dark leaning against a car, leaning against somebody without someone thinking you are bad, without somebody saying it is wrong, without the whole world waiting for you to make a mistake when all you wanted, all you wanted, Sally, was to love and to love and to love and to love, and no one could call that crazy.

Minerva Writes Poems

Minerva is only a little bit older than me but already she has two kids and a husband who left. Her mother raised her kids alone and it looks like her daughters will go that way too. Minerva cries because her luck is unlucky. Every night and every day. And prays. But when the kids are asleep after she's fed them their pancake dinner, she writes poems on little pieces of paper that she folds over and over and holds in her hands a long time, little pieces of paper that smell like a dime.

She lets me read her poems. I let her read mine. She is always sad like a house on fire—always something wrong. She has many troubles, but the big one is her husband who left and keeps leaving.

One day she is through and lets him know enough is enough. Out the door he goes. Clothes, records, shoes. Out the window and the door locked. But that night he comes back and sends a big rock through the window. Then he is sorry and she opens the door again. Same story.

Next week she comes over black and blue and asks what can she do? Minerva. I don't know which way she'll go. There is nothing *I* can do.

Bums
in the Attic

I want a house on a hill like the ones with the gardens where Papa works. We go on Sundays, Papa's day off. I used to go. I don't anymore. You don't like to go out with us, Papa says. Getting too old? Getting too stuck-up, says Nenny. I don't tell them I am ashamed—all of us staring out the window like the hungry. I am tired of looking at what we can't have. When we win the lottery... Mama begins, and then I stop listening.

People who live on hills sleep so close to the stars they forget those of us who live too much on earth. They don't look down at all except to be content to live on hills. They have nothing to do with last week's garbage or fear of rats. Night comes. Nothing wakes them but the wind.

One day I'll own my own house, but I won't forget who I am or where I came from. Passing bums will ask, Can I come in? I'll offer them the attic, ask them to stay, because I know how it is to be without a house.

Some days after dinner, guests and I will sit in front of a fire. Floorboards will squeak upstairs. The attic grumble.

Rats? They'll ask.

Bums, I'll say, and I'll be happy.

Beautiful & Cruel

I am an ugly daughter. I am the one nobody comes for.

Nenny says she won't wait her whole life for a husband to come and get her, that Minerva's sister left her mother's house by having a baby, but she doesn't want to go that way either. She wants things all her own, to pick and choose. Nenny has pretty eyes and it's easy to talk that way if you are pretty.

My mother says when I get older my dusty hair will settle and my blouse will learn to stay clean, but I have decided not to grow up tame like the others who lay their necks on the threshold waiting for the ball and chain.

In the movies there is always one with red red lips who is beautiful and cruel. She is the one who drives the men crazy and laughs them all away. Her power is her own. She will not give it away.

I have begun my own quiet war. Simple. Sure. I am one who leaves the table like a man, without putting back the chair or picking up the plate.

A
Smart Cookie

I could've been somebody, you know? My mother says and sighs. She has lived in this city her whole life. She can speak two languages. She can sing an opera. She knows how to fix a T.V. But she doesn't know which subway train to take to get downtown. I hold her hand very tight while we wait for the right train to arrive.

She used to draw when she had time. Now she draws with a needle and thread, little knotted rosebuds, tulips made of silk thread. Someday she would like to go to the ballet. Someday she would like to see a play. She borrows opera records from the public library and sings with velvety lungs powerful as morning glories.

Today while cooking oatmeal she is Madame Butterfly until she sighs and points the wooden spoon at me. I could've been somebody, you know? Esperanza, you go to school. Study hard. That Madame Butterfly was a fool. She stirs the oatmeal. Look at my *comadres*. She means Izaura whose husband left and Yolanda whose husband is dead. Got to take care all your own, she says shaking her head.

Then out of nowhere:

Shame is a bad thing, you know. It keeps you down. You want to know why I quit school? Because I didn't have nice clothes. No clothes, but I had brains.

Yup, she says disgusted, stirring again. I was a smart cookie then.

What Sally Said

He never hits me hard. She said her mama rubs lard on all the places where it hurts. Then at school she'd say she fell. That's where all the blue places come from. That's why her skin is always scarred.

But who believes her. A girl that big, a girl who comes in with her pretty face all beaten and black can't be falling off the stairs. He never hits me hard.

But Sally doesn't tell about that time he hit her with his hands just like a dog, she said, like if I was an animal. He thinks I'm going to run away like his sisters who made the family ashamed. Just because I'm a daughter, and then she doesn't say.

Sally was going to get permission to stay with us a little and one Thursday she came finally with a sack full of clothes and a paper bag of sweetbread her mama sent. And would've stayed too except when the dark came her father, whose eyes were little from crying, knocked on the door and said please come back, this is the last time. And she said Daddy and went home.

Then we didn't need to worry. Until one day Sally's father catches her talking to a boy and the next day she doesn't come to school. And the next. Until the way Sally tells it, he just went crazy, he just forgot he was her father between the buckle and the belt.

You're not my daughter, you're not my daughter. And then he broke into his hands.

The Monkey Garden

The monkey doesn't live there anymore. The monkey moved—to Kentucky—and took his people with him. And I was glad because I couldn't listen anymore to his wild screaming at night, the twangy yakkety-yak of the people who owned him. The green metal cage, the porcelain table top, the family that spoke like guitars. Monkey, family, table. All gone.

And it was then we took over the garden we had been afraid to go into when the monkey screamed and showed its yellow teeth.

There were sunflowers big as flowers on Mars and thick

cockscombs bleeding the deep red fringe of theater curtains. There were dizzy bees and bow-tied fruit flies turning somersaults and humming in the air. Sweet sweet peach trees. Thorn roses and thistle and pears. Weeds like so many squinty-eyed stars and brush that made your ankles itch and itch until you washed with soap and water. There were big green apples hard as knees. And everywhere the sleepy smell of rotting wood, damp earth and dusty hollyhocks thick and perfumy like the blue-blond hair of the dead.

Yellow spiders ran when we turned rocks over and pale worms blind and afraid of light rolled over in their sleep. Poke a stick in the sandy soil and a few blue-skinned beetles would appear, an avenue of ants, so many crusty lady bugs. This was a garden, a wonderful thing to look at in the spring. But bit by bit, after the monkey left, the garden began to take over itself. Flowers stopped obeying the little bricks that kept them from growing beyond their paths. Weeds mixed in. Dead cars appeared overnight like mushrooms. First one and then another and then a pale blue pickup with the front windshield missing. Before you knew it, the monkey garden became filled with sleepy cars.

Things had a way of disappearing in the garden, as if the garden itself ate them, or, as if with its old-man memory, it put them away and forgot them. Nenny found a dollar and a dead mouse between two rocks in the stone wall where the morning glories climbed, and once when we were playing hide-and-seek, Eddie Vargas laid his head beneath a hibiscus tree and fell asleep there like a Rip Van Winkle until somebody remembered he was in the game and went back to look for him.

This, I suppose, was the reason why we went there. Far away from where our mothers could find us. We and a few old dogs who lived inside the empty cars. We made a clubhouse once on the back of that old blue pickup. And besides, we liked to jump from the roof of one car to another and pretend they were giant mushrooms.

Somebody started the lie that the monkey garden had been there before anything. We liked to think the garden could hide things for a thousand years. There beneath the roots of soggy flowers were the bones of murdered pirates and dinosaurs, the eye of a unicorn turned to coal.

This is where I wanted to die and where I tried one day but not even the monkey garden would have me. It was the last day I would go there.

Who was it that said I was getting too old to play the games? Who was it I didn't listen to? I only remember that when the others ran, I wanted to run too, up and down and through the monkey garden, fast as the boys, not like Sally who screamed if she got her stockings muddy.

I said, Sally, come on, but she wouldn't. She stayed by the curb talking to Tito and his friends. Play with the kids if you want, she said, I'm staying here. She could be stuck-up like that if she wanted to, so I just left.

It was her own fault too. When I got back Sally was pretending to be mad... something about the boys having stolen her keys. Please give them back to me, she said punching the nearest one with a soft fist. They were laughing. She was too. It was a joke I didn't get.

I wanted to go back with the other kids who were still jumping on cars, still chasing each other through the garden, but Sally had her own game.

One of the boys invented the rules. One of Tito's friends said you can't get the keys back unless you kiss us and Sally pretended to be mad at first but she said yes. It was that simple.

I don't know why, but something inside me wanted to throw a stick. Something wanted to say no when I watched Sally going into the garden with Tito's buddies all grinning. It was just a kiss, that's all. A kiss for each one. So what, she said.

Only how come I felt angry inside. Like something wasn't right. Sally went behind that old blue pickup to kiss the boys and get her keys back, and I ran up three flights of stairs to where Tito lived. His mother was ironing shirts. She was sprinkling water on them from an empty pop bottle and smoking a cigarette.

Your son and his friends stole Sally's keys and now they won't give them back unles she kisses them and right now they're making her kiss them, I said all out of breath from the three flights of stairs.

Those kids, she said, not looking up from her ironing.

That's all?

What do you want me to do, she said, call the cops? And kept on ironing.

I looked at her a long time, but couldn't think of anything to say, and ran back down the three flights to the garden where Sally needed to be saved. I took three big sticks and a brick and figured this was enough.

But when I got there Sally said go home. Those boys said leave us alone. I felt stupid with my brick. They all looked at me as if *I* was the one that was crazy and made me feel ashamed.

And then I don't know why but I had to run away. I had to hide myself at the other end of the garden, in the jungle part, under a tree that wouldn't mind if I lay down and cried a long time. I closed my eyes like tight stars so that I wouldn't, but I did. My face felt hot. Everything inside hiccupped.

I read somewhere in India there are priests who can will their heart to stop beating. I wanted to will my blood to stop, my heart to quit its pumping. I wanted to be dead, to turn into the rain, my eyes melt into the ground like two black snails. I wished and wished. I closed my eyes and willed it, but when I got up my dress was green and I had a headache.

I looked at my feet in their white socks and ugly round shoes. They seemed far away. They didn't seem to be my feet anymore. And the garden that had been such a good place to play didn't seem mine either.

Red Clowns

Sally, you lied. It wasn't what you said at all. What he did. Where he touched me. I didn't want it, Sally. The way they said it, the way it's supposed to be, all the storybooks and movies, why did you lie to me?

I was waiting by the red clowns. I was standing by the tilt-a-whirl where you said. And anyway I don't like carnivals. I went to be with you because you laugh on the tilt-a-whirl, you throw your head back and laugh. I hold your change, wave, count how many times you go by. Those boys that look at you because you're pretty. I like to be with you, Sally. You're my friend. But that big boy, where did he take you? I waited such a long time. I waited by the red clowns, just like you said, but you never came, you never came for me.

Sally Sally a hundred times. Why didn't you hear me when I called? Why didn't you tell them to leave me alone? The one who grabbed me by the arm, he wouldn't let me go. He said I love you, Spanish girl, I love you, and pressed his sour mouth to mine.

Sally, make him stop. I couldn't make them go away. I couldn't do anything but cry. I don't remember. It was dark. I don't remember. I don't remember. Please don't make me tell it all.

Why did you leave me all alone? I waited my whole life. You're a liar. They all lied. All the books and magazines, everything that told it wrong. Only his dirty fingernails against my skin, only his sour smell again. The moon that watched. The tilt-a-whirl. The red clowns laughing their thick-tongue laugh.

Then the colors began to whirl. Sky tipped. Their high black gym shoes ran. Sally, you lied, you lied. He wouldn't let me go. He said I love you, I love you, Spanish girl.

Linoleum Roses

Sally got married like we knew she would, young and not ready but married just the same. She met a marshmallow salesman at a school bazaar, and she married him in another state where it's legal to get married before eighth grade. She has her husband and her house now, her pillowcases and her plates. She says she is in love, but I think she did it to escape.

Sally says she likes being married because now she gets to buy her own things when her husband gives her money. She is happy, except sometimes her husband gets angry and once he broke the door where his foot went through, though most days he is okay. Except he won't let her talk on the telephone. And he doesn't let her look out the window. And he doesn't like her friends, so nobody gets to visit her unless he is working.

She sits at home because she is afraid to go outside without his permission. She looks at all the things they own: the towels and the toaster, the alarm clock and the drapes. She likes looking at the walls, at how neatly their corners meet, the linoleum roses on the floor, the ceiling smooth as wedding cake.

The Three Sisters

They came with the wind that blows in August, thin as a spider web and barely noticed. Three who did not seem to be related to anything but the moon. One with laughter like tin and one with eyes of a cat and one with hands like porcelain. The aunts, the three sisters, *las comadres*, they said.

The baby died. Lucy and Rachel's sister. One night a dog cried, and the next day a yellow bird flew in through an open window. Before the week was over, the baby's fever was worse. Then Jesus came and took the baby with him far away. That's what their mother said.

Then the visitors came... in and out of the little house. It was hard to keep the floors clean. Anybody who had ever wondered what color the walls were came and came to look at that little thumb of a human in a box like candy.

I had never seen the dead before, not for real, not in somebody's living room for people to kiss and bless themselves and light a candle for. Not in a house. It seemed strange.

They must've known, the sisters. They had the power and could sense what was what. They said, Come here, and gave me a stick of gum. They smelled like Kleenex or the inside of a satin handbag, and then I didn't feel afraid.

What's your name, the cat-eyed one asked.

Esperanza, I said.

Esperanza, the old blue-veined one repeated in a high thin voice. Esperanza... a good good name.

My knees hurt, the one with the funny laugh complained.

Tomorrow it will rain.

Yes, tomorrow, they said.

How do you know? I asked.

We know.

Look at her hands, cat-eyed said.

And they turned them over and over as if they were looking for something.

She's special.

Yes, she'll go very far.

Yes, yes, hmmm.

Make a wish.

A wish?

Yes, make a wish. What do you want?

Anything? I said.

Well, why not?

I closed my eyes.

Did you wish already?

Yes, I said.

Well, that's all there is to it. It'll come true.

How do you know? I asked.

We know, we know.

Esperanza. The one with marble hands called me aside. Esperanza. She held my face with her blue-veined hands and looked and looked at me. A long silence. When you leave you must remember always to come back, she said.

What?

When you leave you must remember to come back for the others. A circle, understand? You will always be Esperanza. You will always be Mango Street. You can't erase what you know. You can't forget who you are.

Then I didn't know what to say. It was as if she could read my mind, as if she knew what I had wished for, and I felt ashamed for having made such a selfish wish.

You must remember to come back. For the ones who cannot leave as easily as you. You will remember? She asked as if she was telling me. Yes, yes, I said a little confused.

Good, she said, rubbing my hands. Good. That's all. You can go.

I got up to join Lucy and Rachel who were already outside waiting by the door, wondering what I was doing talking to three old ladies who smelled like cinnamon. I didn't understand everything they had told me. I turned around. They smiled and waved in their smoky way.

Then I didn't see them. Not once, or twice, or ever again.

Alicia & I Talking on Edna's Steps

I like Alicia because once she gave me a little leather purse with the word GUADALAJARA stitched on it, which is home for Alicia, and one day she will go back there. But today she is listening to my sadness because I don't have a house.

You live right here, 4006 Mango, Alicia says and points to the house I am ashamed of.

No, this isn't my house I say and shake my head as if shaking could undo the year I've lived here. I don't belong. I don't ever want to come from here. You have a home, Alicia, and one day you'll go there, to a town you remember, but me

I never had a house, not even a photograph... Only one I dream of.

No, Alicia says. Like it or not you are Mango Street, and one day you'll come back too.

Not me. Not until somebody makes it better.

Who's going to do it? The mayor?

And the thought of the mayor coming to Mango Street makes me laugh out loud.

Who's going to do it? Not the mayor.

A House of My Own

Not a flat. Not an apartment in back. Not a man's house. Not a daddy's. A house all my own. With my porch and my pillow, my pretty purple petunias. My books and my stories. My two shoes waiting beside the bed. Nobody to shake a stick at. Nobody's garbage to pick up after.

Only a house quiet as snow, a space for myself to go, clean as paper before the poem.

Mango Says Goodbye Sometimes

I like to tell stories. I tell them inside my head. I tell them after the mailman says, Here's your mail. Here's your mail he said.

I make a story for my life, for each step my brown shoe takes. I say, "And so she trudged up the wooden stairs, her sad brown shoes taking her to the house she never liked."

I like to tell stories. I am going to tell you a story about a girl who didn't want to belong.

We didn't always live on Mango Street. Before that we lived on Loomis on the third floor, and before that we lived on Keeler. Before Keeler it was Paulina, but what I remember most is Mango Street, sad red house, the house I belong but do not belong to.

I put it down on paper and then the ghost does not ache so much. I write it down and Mango says goodbye sometimes. She does not hold me with both arms. She sets me free.

One day I will pack my bags of books and paper. One day I will say goodbye to Mango. I am too strong for her to keep me here forever. One day I will go away.

Friends and neighbors will say. What happened to that Esperanza? Where did she go with all those books and paper? Why did she march so far away?

They will not know I have gone away to come back. For the ones I left behind. For the ones who cannot out.

他们的感想

漫步芒果街

导读

黄梅

《芒果街上的小屋》(1984)是美国当代女诗人桑德拉·希斯内罗丝(Sandra Cisneros, 1954—)的成名作。

关于作者

希斯内罗丝是墨西哥移民的女儿,六十年代在芝加哥的移民社区里长大,受政府资助上了大学,后来又因写作天赋而被推荐进了国际知名的爱荷华大学研究生写作班,毕业后当过中学教师和大学辅导员,与少数族裔的贫困学生打了很多交道。看到他们的困境和迷惘,她联想到自己的成长历程,决定要写点什么。一部《芒果街》酝酿了五年,成书在她三十岁时,采用一种诗歌与小说的混合文体,讲述一个少女的成长,描绘移民群落的生存状况。

在20世纪后期美国知识界高度重视族裔问题的文化氛围里,这本书引起了相当大的反响和争论。1984年出版,次年便获得了"前哥伦布基金会"颁发的美国图书奖,又陆续进入大中小学课堂,后来大出版社兰登书屋取得了版权并推出其平装本。与此同时,各种评论、导读纷纷出台,耶鲁大学的大牌文学教授哈罗德·布鲁姆也亲自出马编了一本导读。有些导读十分详细,书里的字句被条分缕析,挖掘隐义。如此对待一本并不引经据典,没有文学野心的半"童书",的确有些令人惊讶,可以说是当代美国文化的特异景观。

少女呢喃

喃喃自语是少女埃斯佩朗莎·科尔德罗的存在方式之一。

《芒果街》全书由 44 节短小的片段独白构成。每节围绕一个不同的话题。那些"节"或"篇"讲述在小埃斯佩朗莎心中留下痕迹的一些经历,或围绕某事某人,或有关头发、云朵、树木和荒园,等等。

进入芒果街世界,我们首先接触的就是那讲话的声音。人们常用"清澈如水"之类的词汇来形容它。尽管它其实并不像乍读时感觉的那么纯粹而明澈,尽管渐渐地我们会分辨出复合于其中的成年人的追怀之情,但是最主要也给人最深印象的,确实还是那个十多岁的敏感小女孩的话音。小埃斯佩朗莎在对自己、对自己想象中的至亲好友说话,心口相通,毫不设防,没有间隔和距离。

"我们先前不住芒果街。先前我们住鲁米斯的三楼。再先前我们住吉勒……"开篇那近乎透明的语句直接把我们带进科尔德罗们的生活。

不时的,有句子会像阳光下闪着异样光彩的石子出其不意地吸引了我们的注意力。在这样的时刻我们不妨稍稍驻足,听听那些字句的音调,品品它们所提示的意象。比如:芒果街的新居"它很小,是红色的,门前一方窄台阶,窗户小得让你觉得它们像是在屏着呼吸。几处墙砖蚀成了粉。前门那么鼓,你要用力推才进得来。"屏住呼吸的窗户和鼓胀的门。多么栩栩如生。什么样的人会这么看这么想?那拟人的笔法所展示的难道不是个万物有生命有灵魂的童话世界?当然,新颖而生动的比喻所提示的感受却不一定简单也不一定轻松:小窗口很可能意味着压抑,与肿胀相关的首先是疼痛,如此等等。

再比如"头发"一篇中,写到一家六口每个人的头发都不一样。但只有"妈妈的头发,妈妈的头发,好像一朵朵小小的玫瑰花结,一枚枚小小的糖果圈儿……把鼻子伸进去闻一闻吧……气味又那么香甜。是那种待烤的面包暖暖的香味,是那种她给你让出一角被窝时,和着体温散发的芬芳。"这里,中译相当妥帖而传神地转达了原作的风格。作者用的是简单稚拙的儿童语言,没有抽象观念,没有复合长句,一个又一个逗号断开了又串联起那些日常的小词(头发糖果被窝之类)和鲜活的意象,三五词一顿的明快节奏和着音步的抑扬,构成一曲母爱的颂歌。从头发的外观到气味再到对母亲的依偎,行文恰如女孩的思绪轻盈跳动。

还有那些歌谣……

在这些诗意的片刻,短暂的停留曾把我带回到凝神注视疏疏坠落的雨滴一点一点打湿北京四合庭院地面砖头的年月。那是很多年以前的事了——记忆的天空里依稀地布着夏日的树荫。不同读者的感受肯定是不一样的,但不论是青少年还是成年人,如果读得慢一点,让埃斯佩朗莎的轻声呢喃在你的心镜中投映出某些图像,呼唤出某些联想,敲打出某些节奏和音律的回声,那将会是一种美的体验——即使其中有时会包含痛楚和酸涩。

背后的"故事"

《芒果街》虽然由一些相对独立的小"节"构成,但它们有内在的关联,总和起来讲述了一个关于美国大城市中贫苦墨西哥裔少女成长的"故事"。在"我的名字"一节里,埃斯佩朗莎说明:她那多音节的长名字来自西班牙语,在美国学校里被同学认为既别扭又滑稽。她很明白:自己属于"棕色的人"。

在种族差异和矛盾非常突出、对肤色和族裔问题十分敏感的美国社会,身为拉丁美洲移民后代常常意味着家境贫穷、遭人歧视以及文化上的隔阂与失落。因此,埃斯佩朗莎的成长历程蕴含丰富的社会学内容。布鲁姆主编的导读也主要聚焦于与作者身份和作品内容相关的族裔、性别、贫富和文化差异等问题。

初到芒果街,小埃斯佩朗莎结交的头一个朋友是"猫皇后凯茜"。凯茜家里群猫聚集,连餐桌上都有猫自由散步,显然也是穷人家庭,决算不上讲究。小凯茜对新来的邻家女孩很友善,主动给她介绍当地街坊和店铺。然而她也会吹嘘自家的法国亲戚和那里的"家宅",会童言无忌地直说科尔德罗之流(非白人)的到来导致社区档次下降,所以她家将要向北迁居,还会警告新来者不要和"像老鼠一样邋邋遢遢的"露西姐妹玩耍。小孩子似懂非懂的话充分地并且残忍地折射着成人社会的矛盾、弊端和偏见。

透过小埃斯佩朗莎的眼我们认识了众多芒果街的拉美移民。有凯茜走后搬进她家房子的"么么"一家。有住在他家地下室的波多黎各人——他们中的一名少年曾偷来一辆黄色凯迪拉克豪华车并载上所有邻家孩子在窄街上兜风过了把瘾,然后被警察拘捕进了局子。有又想攒钱和波多黎各男友结婚又想在美国另找个阔丈夫的玛琳。有被男人遗弃的单身母亲法加斯:她带一大窝孩子艰难谋生,无人管教的小家伙们一味胡闹,终于有一天酿成惨祸。还有新到美国来的胖女人玛玛西塔,她不肯下楼也不愿说英语……

一顿午餐也能告诉我们许多事情。小埃斯佩朗莎眼巴巴地看着那些能在学校吃午饭的"特殊的孩子",无比向往,千方百计说服了妈妈给她带饭,却遭到嬷嬷的拦阻,委屈地哭了起来,勉强留下来后,她在其实"没什么特别"的食堂里流着泪吃带来的冷腻的米饭三明治(她家的午饭没有肉),感到那么失望,那么满心屈辱。我们恐怕得动用点想象力才能充分体会学校食堂对于这个孩子的巨大诱惑。把如此微不足道的就餐权利幻化成某种美好辉煌体验的,该是多么辛酸而卑微的处境。此外,从各位掌事嬷嬷的言行,我们还能感受到拉美裔穷孩子读书的天主教会学校的氛围。

当然,穷孩子也有自己的快乐。埃斯佩朗莎不顾凯茜的警告,和露西姐妹交了朋友。她们凑钱合伙买了一辆旧自行车,三人一起挤上去,风驰电掣地穿过整个街区。那是"我们的好日子"。老吉尔的旧家具店又小又黑又脏,里面只有些破破烂烂的东西,但对孩子们来说仍然魅力无穷——比如那个能发出奇妙声音的音乐盒。仰头看云彩是大自然提供的探讨"科学"和"审美"的机会。唱着歌谣跳绳则是街头平民孩子的快乐游戏。

参加小表弟的洗礼晚会是忧喜参半的体验。妈妈为埃斯佩朗莎买一身鲜亮的新裙子,却没买新鞋。这让她沮丧万分,晚会上根本不敢去和男孩子跳舞。不过,墨西哥移民中存在着浓浓的家族和同乡亲情。长者会关照孩子们,而且大家沾边不沾边都算是"表亲"。后来埃斯佩朗莎在拿乔叔叔的鼓励和邀请下进了舞场,跳得兴高采烈,无比风光。

发生化蛹为蝶巨变的青春期不知不觉就来到了。小姑娘们开始注意自己的屁股和腰身。她们跳着舞,跳着绳,同时半是天真无邪、半是初解风情地唱着歌谣。她们穿上别人送的五颜六色的旧高跟鞋招摇过市。她们开始对男孩子生出兴趣。埃斯佩朗莎开始打第一份零工。她在照相馆分装照片,那儿的一个看来和气谦卑的东方人突然吻了她。我们几乎能听到她的心跳,感到她的尴尬和惊恐,也不免会对留在叙述之外的那东方人的境遇、心态和动机等等生出一些模糊的猜度。真正的初吻发生在这之后。在嘉年华会游乐场上,约定碰头的女友萨莉没露面,却有一群男孩来纠缠,其中一个白人少年还强行亲吻了埃斯佩朗莎,打破了她对爱情的幻想。

然而,不论有多少压力,有多少挫折和伤害,埃斯佩朗莎会像她家房子近旁那四棵细弱的小树一样突破砖石的阻挠顽强成长。她每天都和它们对话:"它们的力量是个秘密。它们在地下展开凶猛的根系。它们向上生长也向下生长,用它们须发样的脚趾攥紧泥土,用它们猛烈的牙齿噬咬天空……"这般有如猛兽的树是不可阻挡的。能在痛苦时刻思考树的秘密的小埃斯佩朗莎也一定是打不垮的。她要长大,有一天要离开芒果街。

离开意味着更有意义的归来——如伴随八月的风一起来临的三个老姐妹所告诫的:"你离开时要记得为了其他人回来……你不能忘记你知道的事情。你不能忘记你是谁。"如果说离开芒果街的渴望几乎等于对成功和富裕的追求,那么返回芒果街的责任和期许则在本质上超越了通常意义上的美国梦。

如许多评论者所强调,这本书的另一个重要关注点是性别问题。有人说《芒果街》中的男性形象统统不佳,但事实并非如此。半夜醒来的疲惫的父亲、聚会中善解人意的拿乔叔叔,还有许多别的挣扎着谋生养家的男人,勾勒他们的笔显然是饱含同情的。当然，那同一支笔也毫不含糊地写出了萨莉、密涅瓦们的父亲或丈夫殴打女性的劣迹，写出了墨西哥裔男人的种种陈旧或荒唐的性别观念和行为方式——因为那些也是芒果街生活的一部分。

在一节节亲切的讲述中，我们听到了小埃斯佩朗莎对男孩女孩差异的非常具体而感性的分辨，体会到她因家庭主妇(包括她母亲和鹭鸶儿们)被荒废的才华而生出的惋惜，还见证了她对玛琳和萨莉以嫁人为中心的人生设计的审视和最终扬弃，如此等等。这些是成长中的女孩子关心的问题，也是已经成年的女性仍在思考的问题。可以说，幸运的是，作者的艺术直觉让她没有过于主题先行，没有脱离具体真切的生活经验。因此，展现在读者面前的，不是有关社会性别的说教，而是美国墨西哥裔少女的色彩斑斓的生活画卷。

梦想

房子是小埃斯佩朗莎的梦想，也是全书的核心象征。关于房子的梦想中也包含了对理想自我的憧憬。在书中许多处拟人化的描写中，比如关于房子、气球和树木的意象，都可以看出主人公的自我感觉在客观世界的投影。这本小说，从某种意义上说,是关于一个人在世界上寻求自我,寻找一片归属之地的故事。

> 他们[父母]一直对我们说,有一天,我们会搬进一所房子,一所真正的大屋……我们的房子会有自来水和好用的水管。里面还有真正的楼梯。不是门厅台阶,而是像电视上的房子里那样的楼梯……

定义梦想的一个关键词组是"像电视上的"。科尔德罗一家希望住进电视上展示的那种房子,固然表明他们想摆脱贫困、分享美好生活,但从中也可分明看出大众媒体所代表的强势文化和主流生活方式"洗脑"的作用。

梦想和愿望并非凭空而来。我们记得那位一直坚持"别说英语"的玛玛西塔。让她心碎的是:她自己的小儿子开口说的第一句话就是英语,他会唱的头一支曲子是百事可乐的广告歌。听英语广告歌长大的孩子会怎样梦想将来的生活?与此类似,还有准备赴晚会的小埃斯佩朗莎对新鞋子的重视。为什么她那么强烈地渴望与新衣相配的新鞋子呢?为什么一双旧鞋就让她羞惭得连脚都不敢伸出来了呢?轻灵的叙述只蜻蜓点水般地提到了男孩子的注视。然而我们若是在那些隐含的问号旁稍许驻留,就能感受到少年经验背后的近乎沉重的成人"潜台词"。是的,商业化社会里人们以消费品来定义的"美"和"体面"的标准多么霸道地主宰了孩子的感觉!与朦胧的性觉醒纠缠在一起的那种把自己物化成男性欲望对象的心理过程又是多么"自然"地发生在天真少女身上!

随着小埃斯佩朗莎渐渐长大,她的梦中房子不断有所变化。她羡慕"住在山上、睡得靠星星如此近的人",但是也明确意识到,那些高高在上的人"忘记了我们这些住在地面上的人。"于是,她想:有一天她自己在山上有了房子,要在阁楼里收留无家可归的流浪者。接近收尾之处,在"一所我自己的房子"中,她再一次描述了心目中的房子:

> 不是小公寓。也不是阴面的大公寓。也不是哪一个男人的房子。也不是爸爸的。是完完全全我自己的……
> 只是一所寂静如雪的房子,一个自己归去的空间,洁净如同诗笔未落的纸。

这时,如诗的语言构筑起的房子承载的是更加成熟的埃斯佩朗莎的精神追求,小节标题也显然在有意识地回应维吉尼亚·吴尔夫的名篇《自己的一间屋》。不过,它们传达的,很可能仍只是某一特定时段的感受,而非最终的结论。

在这个意义上,我们庆幸小埃斯佩朗莎在成长中不断修订着丰富着自己的梦,而且有代表墨西哥土著文化的女巫般的神秘人物指点她。梦想是人前行和创造的动力。然而梦想也是需要甄别,需要分析,需要批判和修正的。

让我们就在"梦想"的音符上结束这篇导读。

对众多年轻的和已经不再年轻的初读者和再读者,这都是一本开卷有益的书,既可以成为一种文学体验,也可以唤起情感的交流和共鸣;既可以当做自己试笔写作的参照,也可以触发对人生和社会的体察与深思。

请缓步徜徉于《芒果街》。

青芒果之味

沈胜衣

芝加哥的拉美裔聚居区，贫穷，拥挤，吵闹，单调。欢笑是那样单薄，梦想是那样邈远。小女孩埃斯佩朗莎认识一位爱美爱打扮的萨莉，她家里管教很严，放学得直接回家。那时候，"你变成了一个不同的萨莉。你把裙子拉直。你擦去了眼皮上的蓝色眼影。你不笑，萨莉。""萨莉，你有时会希望自己可以不回家吗？你希望有一天你的脚可以走呀走，把你远远地带出芒果街……"

埃斯佩朗莎自己的屋前有四棵细瘦的树儿，她"每晚对着树说话"。"它们是唯一懂得我的。我是唯一懂得它们的。"她想要"一所我自己的房子"。"没有别人扔下的垃圾要拾起。""只是一所寂静如雪的房子，一个自己归去的空间，洁净如同诗笔未落的纸。"

后来，她终于走出了芒果街，有了自己亮紫色的房子。但她忘不了从前那段时光，用"诗笔"写下了一本《芒果街上的小屋》。在现实中，她的名字是桑德拉·希斯内罗丝，这本"诗小说"，以优美、敏感而细腻的文笔，写出一个女孩的成长，微尘般的快乐和阴影般的困窘,观察与思悟,幻想与疼痛。

在芒果街上那悲哀的红色小屋里外的众生相:

爷爷去世了,勇敢的爸爸哭了。"黑暗里醒来的疲惫的爸爸。""我想要是我自己的爸爸死去了我会做什么。于是我把爸爸抱在怀里,我要抱啊抱啊抱住他。"

孩子们在看云,聊着各种云都像些什么。"在天空下睡去,醒来又沉醉。在你忧伤的时候,天空会给你安慰。可是忧伤太多,天空不够。蝴蝶也不够,花儿也不够。大多数美的东西都不够。"

因长得美而被丈夫锁在屋里的拉菲娜,"年纪轻轻就因为倚在窗口太久太久而变老"。"酒吧的乐声从街角传来,拉菲娜希望能在变老以前去那里,去跳舞。"

"玛琳,街灯下独自起舞的人,在某个地方唱着同一首歌。""她在等一辆小汽车停下来,等着一颗星星坠落,等一个人改变她的生活。"

……

这些卑微的人,上帝很忙,没空照看他们,让他们在人间一再摔倒。

也有"好日子"的乐趣。几个小孩凑钱买了一辆自行车,一起骑着在街上快乐地兜圈。有个胖女人说:你们的装载量很大呀。小孩喊道:你的装载量也很大呀。

也有人情的慰藉。洗礼晚会,她有了新衣服,可是还缺鞋子。穿着旧凉鞋的她不敢和别人跳舞,拿乔叔叔安慰她说:"你是这里最漂亮的姑娘",拉她跳了舞……

读这些细碎的故事,感觉跟我钟爱的西班牙作家阿索林有共通的气息:都是短小的篇幅,温和的笔墨,写幽微的人与事,平静白描中的忧伤和哀怜。也许,因为他们来自同一个遥远的文化源头?所以汪曾祺、南星对阿索林的两句评语,对桑德拉·希斯内罗丝也是适用的:作品,"像是覆盖着阴影的小溪";其人,有"正视着不可挽救的悲哀的人世间而充满了爱心的目光"。

桑德拉·希斯内罗丝写到一个怀念家乡的玛玛西塔,拒绝说和听英语。而她给书中叙述者取的名字"埃斯佩朗莎",在英语里的意思是"希望",在西班牙语里则"意味着哀伤,意味着等待","一种泥泞的色彩"。这是一个意味深长的象征。作为进入美国的移民,族裔传统文化与现实世界之间,有痛苦的割裂、抗拒,也有痛苦的妥协、追求。

他们要挣扎逃离出那片带着色彩的泥泞,哪怕用最脆弱的笔和诗。埃斯佩朗莎写了一首诗:"我想成为 / 海里的浪,风中的云,/ 但我还只是小小的我。/ 有一天我要 / 跳出自己的身躯……"垂死的卢佩婶婶说:"很好。非常好。""记住你要写下去,你一定要写下去。那会让你自由……"

然而,自由并不意味着摆脱。别人对这小女孩说:"你永远是芒果街的人。你不能忘记你知道的事情。你不能忘记你是谁。""你要记得回来。为了那些不像你那么容易离开的人。"最终,作者在全书结束时说:"我离开是为了回来。为了那些我留在身后的人。为了那些无法出去的人。"

那些身后的人,是桑德拉·希斯内罗丝永远的支撑。但,我们也不能把《芒果街上的小屋》仅仅视为美国种族文化冲突的故事,它属于整个现代世界,我读此书,就不期然想到现在我们城市里的外来人聚居区。

而书中的小女孩,又让我想起老狼唱的:"我像每个恋爱的孩子一样,在大街上琴弦上寂寞成长",想起自己的小时候……

所以,它更是一个生命的故事。

离开,是为了回来。因为过早品尝了未成熟的青芒果,那味道,酸涩却又带着一缕淡淡的幽香,成长的滋味,会始终飘绕在你的生命里,告诉你:你总会离开,你总要回来。

二〇〇五年十二月二十四日,平安夜

那些幸福的小雨点

张悦然

读《芒果街上的小屋》是在一个温暖的冬天。我像是跟随一个欢快的吉卜赛舞者,又像被阿里阿德涅的线团牵着,走进了一座丰饶曲折的地下迷宫。我们穿越屏风相隔的回廊,在一段段摇曳多姿的风景中逗留。我永远不知道接下来要去哪儿,这迷宫将通向何处。唯一明确的是,它是麦芒和番薯的颜色,与童年和故乡连着。

确切地说,这本小书所记录的,是从女孩蜕变为女人的过程,是少女时代的最后的一段光阴。它就像熟透的芒果一般,饱满多汁,任何轻微的碰撞都会留下印迹。在书中,女孩敏感的触角几乎伸向生活的每个角落,妈妈、婶婶、一朵小云彩、一只小狗、一次小伤心、一点小悸动……在少女澄澈的眼底,这些都是打上了"家"和"回忆"的记号的,是完全属于她的。这种确认是很迷人的,因为我们走在成长的路上,越来越畏怯,越来越忧虑,我们曾笃信的事物被怀疑了,我们曾憧憬的事物看不见了,这样一路走来，我们还能确认什么呢？什么是"我"的？是"我"知道、不会失去、不会变迁、不会遗忘的呢？在长大之后，我们之中，又有谁还有一个自己的王国？

令读者感到欣喜的是，这还是一个诗情画意的王国。作者希斯内罗丝将她的跳跃灵动的诗性发挥得淋漓尽致。这种诗性，并不是通过华丽的词藻，对仗的句子弥散开来的。事实上，若你留心一下这本书中的词句（一个微小的建议：当你阅读这本书中的句子时，最好可以读出声来），就会发现，书中没有什么繁赘，都是简单得不能再简单的词和句。每个词句的出现，绝不是一根随意摆放的树枝，它们是有方向的箭，直指靶心——那么精准和有力。当然，它们同时是诙谐机智的。"雪糕一样的厚嘴唇"，"她的气味是粉红的"，"野草多得像眯眼睛的星星"……书中充满了这样诱人的比喻，使希斯内罗丝建造的这座童话王国，绝不逊于她钟爱的名作《爱丽丝镜中奇遇记》。

读这本书的过程中，我几次联想到一位长于捕捉少女神态、举止的画家，巴尔蒂斯。有趣的是，巴尔蒂斯在1929年到1933年间，画过两幅作品，都命名为《街》。有几句分析《街》的评论文字说得很好，我想它同时也回答了我为什么喜欢希斯内罗丝的《芒果街》："那是一种不寻常的梦。在这种梦中，日常生活和寻常事物都只有一点不寻常;在这种梦里,琐碎的日常细节诡异地戏弄着我们的眼睛。"是的,我们必须承认,希斯内罗丝的《芒果街》还有一点怪,这是它使我们兴奋又不安的原因。

我一向很羡慕能将少女描摹得细致入微,生动明艳的艺术家,比如巴尔蒂斯,比如希斯内罗丝。因为这些活泼的作品,将帮他们抓住青春,留住韶华光阴中一抹永不褪色的颜彩。于是,他们不再会衰老,在阴雨连连的日子里,只要将这犹如压箱绸缎般的宝物拿出来,幽暗的房间里登时光芒四射,再黯淡的人也会在瞬息间被点亮。他们在雨中跳舞,快乐得像个孩子。孩子,是的,孩子就是那些在雨中热切地伸出双手,接住雨水的人。他们想更多一点地触摸世界,于是他们自己伸出手来要。就是那么简单。

很高兴提前读到这样一本好书,由衷地感谢它的作者希斯内罗丝,是她让我们蒙着这些幸福的小雨点,雀跃一如孩子。同时我们也许还应该感谢此书睿智的译者,潘帕,他对原文的深刻的领悟以及高超的文字驾驭能力,都使这本书增色不少。据说他是个隐世的才子,偶有兴致,翻译些自己喜欢的文字。于是有了这本他翻译的佳作,谢谢他。

二〇〇六年二月三日于北京

感谢

编者

  所以要用博尔赫斯的诗句来做题记，一是因为《芒果街》的西班牙语文学源流；二是因为诗人博尔赫斯同时也擅长制造诗歌与小说的混血文字，而《芒果街》正是一部具有诗歌属性的小说；更因为，那许多个短篇，如一霎一霎细雨，洗亮了读它的人的记忆庭园。

  现在我要来提一提让这翩然细雨落在中文读者眼前的人，感谢这些因一本好书的机缘而汇聚起来的热诚与好心。

  先是我的师弟何宁，是他在国外时看到这本书，向我推荐；在译者潘帕的博客里，我看到过当今最好的文艺类读书笔记。庆幸是由他来接受这样一项冒险：忍受翻译过程的拘束，传达原文纤细灵动的特质。也庆幸有插图作者友雅,富于梦幻感的画面很好地衬托了文字。接下来，黄梅老师、何宁、肖毛、谢山青和我的其他同事通读了草稿并提出了细致的修改意见。还有第一批读到它并写下赞美文字的人,也就是本书的序跋评的作者。借助他们的名望和文字魅力,书可以为更多人所知。其中,《英汉大词典》主编陆谷孙先生经再三邀请,加之受到向读者推荐好书的责任感驱使,拨冗夜读,亲撰译本序,殊为难得;老翻译家李文俊先生也欣然命笔,写来千字趣文;学者黄梅以一贯严谨细致的文风写下长文作为导读;作家沈胜衣选择平安夜来为它构筑佳评;作家毛尖和张悦然则出于对原著和潘帕文字的双重喜爱,甚至把这本书当成自己的作品一样来推荐。

还有许多我限于篇幅不曾提到名字的人,在各种细节上给予了帮助和建议,时常成为我的信心和动力之源。

文章乃天成,妙手偶得之,说的不仅是本书的作者,也是上面说到的这些人,因为他们妙手相援,才促成了一本好书的出版。

希望雨继续落,在更多人的眼前,洗亮前尘,带去希望、热爱和幸福的感觉。

图书在版编目（CIP）数据

芒果街上的小屋：英汉对照／（美）桑德拉·希斯内罗丝（Sandra Cisneros）著；潘帕译. —南京：译林出版社，2020.7（2025.6重印）
书名原文：The House on Mango Street
ISBN 978-7-5447-8179-4

Ⅰ.①芒… Ⅱ.①桑…②潘… Ⅲ.①英语－汉语－对照读物②长篇小说－小说集－美国－现代 Ⅳ.①H319.4：I

中国版本图书馆CIP数据核字（2020）第049632号

The House on Mango Street (La Casa en Mango Street) (Renewal) by Sandra Cisneros
Copyright © 1994 by Sandra Cisneros
This edition arranged with Susan Bergholz Literary Services
through Big Apple Agency, Inc., Labuan, Malaysia
Bilingual (Chinese and English) edition copyright © 2020 by Yilin Press, Ltd
All rights reserved.

著作权合同登记号　图字：10-2019-702号

芒果街上的小屋　[美] 桑德拉·希斯内罗丝　／著　潘　帕　／译

责任编辑　　於　梅
装帧设计/插图　友　雅
责任印制　　颜　亮

原文出版　　Random House, 1991
出版发行　　译林出版社
地　　址　　南京市湖南路1号A楼
邮　　箱　　yilin@yilin.com
网　　址　　www.yilin.com
市场热线　　025-86633278
排　　版　　南京展望文化发展有限公司
印　　刷　　南京爱德印刷有限公司
开　　本　　889毫米×1194毫米　1/32
印　　张　　10.5
版　　次　　2020年7月第1版
印　　次　　2025年6月第9次印刷
书　　号　　ISBN 978-7-5447-8179-4
定　　价　　49.00元

版权所有·侵权必究
译林版图书若有印装错误可向出版社调换。质量热线：025-83658316